BY JJ CARROLL

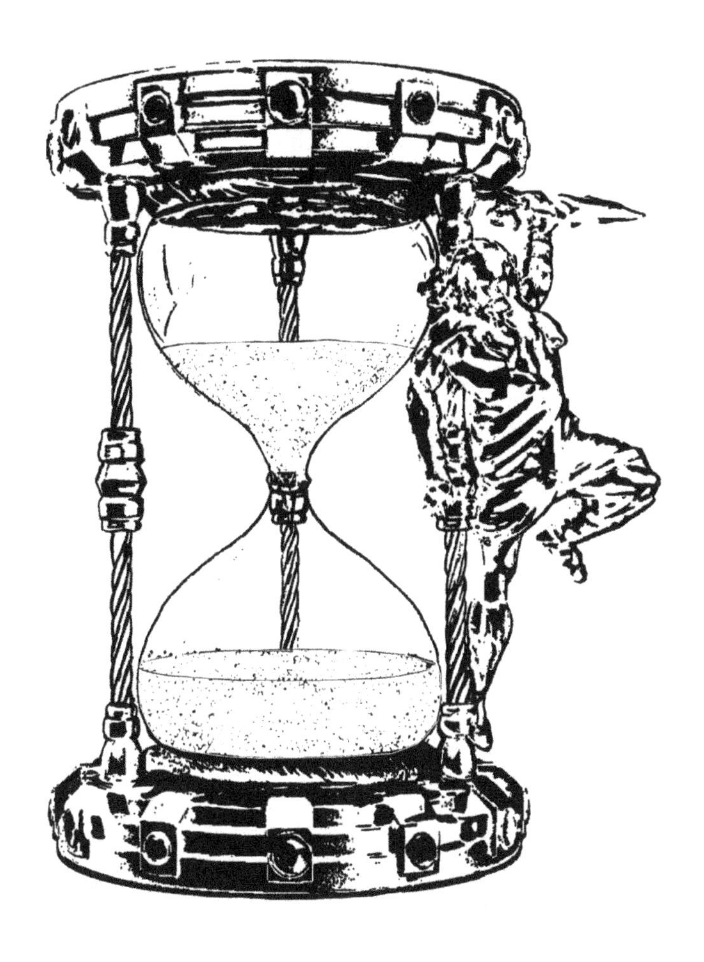

First Published in the United States by Jackson Marbles, an imprint of Quality Business Communications, Inc., Birdsboro, Pennsylvania, USA. 2022

Illustrations by Steve Simoneaux, Fantastic Ink & Magic.

Library of Congress Control Number: 2022933355

Names: Carroll, J. J., author.

Title: Displaced: both feet in the game / by J.J. Carroll.

Description: Birdsboro, PA: Jackson Marbles, an imprint of Quality Business Communications, Inc., 2022. | Summary: A seventh grade virtual reality gamer from 2076 goes on a time-traveling, villain-dodging rescue mission where he could end up trapped in the past forever.

Identifiers: LCCN: 2022933355 | ISBN: 978-1-7328147-2-1 (hardcover) | 978-1-7328147-0-7 (paperback) | 978-1-7328147-1-4 (epub)

Subjects: LCSH Time-travel--Juvenile fiction. | Video games--Juvenile fiction. | United States--History--20th century--Juvenile fiction. | Adventure fiction. | Science fiction. | BISAC JUVENILE FICTION / Science Fiction / Time Travel | JUVENILE FICTION / Historical / United States / 20th Century | JUVENILE FICTION / Action & Adventure / General Classification: LCC PZ7.1.C4178 Dis 2022 | DDC [Fic]--dc23

First edition.

For Reilly, Elizabeth, Isabella, Osiris, Tosin, Brenna, Cameron, Matthew, Raegan and Alexis. Never stop dreaming. Never stop playing the game. There's time enough for all things.

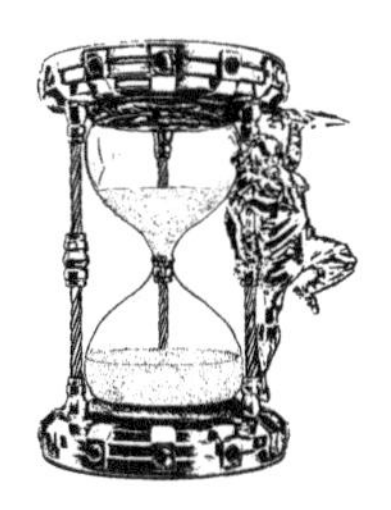

A steaming mass of seventh grade pulp

There he is! *Rex*. The full grown tyrannosaur blocks the entrance to Eniac's Tech Emporium. My best friend, Dingus, elbows me. "Nikola." he whispers. "That is the coolest thing I ever saw!"

Rex's razor sharp bicuspids gleam in the sunlight. His massive feet thunder up and down the sidewalk while the gathered crowd of kids laugh and scream at the sight. One kid pushes his friend into the tyrannosaur's path. Rex opens his mouth to eat the boy, but a girl dashes past and jumps right into the open jaws. A moment later, she emerges unharmed from behind the tyrannosaur squealing with delight to her friends.

Rex is the most highly anticipated virtual reality game of the summer of 2076. But, the game won't go on sale until after the annual Fourth of July Viarbox tournament. That is twenty-one hours and forty-six minutes away. This is just an advertisement.

I wait until Rex's back is turned before I grab Dingus by the shirt and pull him through the onlookers and into the busy store. A bell jingles over our heads as we enter. I go straight to the accessories wall, grab a Viarbox earpiece, and plant myself in line to pay for it.

Dingus goes to his favorite spot at the candy counter. He reaches out and touches a pack of Bleeding Hearts. When the virtual copy appears in his hand, he tears open the pack and pops one into his mouth. Foaming red goo oozes out the side of his mouth. He walks up to a lady and says, "Excuse me. Do I have something in my teeth?" The woman humphs and turns away.

I mentally urge the line to move faster before he gets me into trouble. Dingus is my Viarbox virtual best friend – my only friend – that I got two years ago for my tenth birthday. He's the brother I always wanted, programmed to like me no matter what. I know without a shadow of a doubt that I can put my life in Dingus' hands. But mostly, he gets me into trouble.

Like now.

After he finishes the Bleeding Heart, Dingus touches a Flaming Cyborg to make a virtual copy. He stands next to the same lady while sucking on the candy. She inches away. He inches closer. Once free of its candy shell, the Cyborg in Dingus' mouth shouts in a hysterical voice, informing the lady that she is untrustworthy, fails to bathe regularly, and really needs to stop looking people directly in the eyes.

"Stop that!" the woman yells.

"What?" Dingus says, his voice smooth with innocence. Then he pops another Cyborg into his mouth.

I make it to the checkout where Mr. Eniac raises an eyebrow at Dingus before looking at me. "I know, I know," I say. "I'm sorry." I stick my thumb to the payment plate, snatch up my package and swing by the candy counter. Then I grab Dingus' sleeve and yank him out the door.

We have to duck behind Rex and the crowd of kids, but we make it past unnoticed and head for the corner. I am just opening my mouth to scold Dingus when I feel a thick, heavy splat on my back. A second later, I smell it.

"A puke bomb!" Dingus yells, unnecessarily.

Puke bombs look and smell like real puke. And they stick like glue to whatever they touch. This one is stuck to the back of my shirt. I turn around to see who fired it.

Daemon Digeratti! He's dressed to intimidate and it's working. I'm just a helpless little freckled kid with a chubby virtual best friend. Daemon is tall, mean and has a seven-foot virtual henchman named Kluge. I didn't know he knew I existed. Kids call him Daemon Digerotten when he's not in the room. I'd say you don't want to get on Daemon's bad side, but since he doesn't have a good side, obscurity is best.

His launcher is already loaded with another puke bomb. He smiles and aims it at my head. "That was my mother your stupid *toy* was messing with!"

Oh no! The last time someone called Dingus the "T" word, I was grounded for a week from the resulting damage.

We need to get out of here. Fast.

I quickly size up the situation: We're at the corner. Traffic is turned on full force, both on the ground and in the air. Daemon is about 15 feet away, closer to the store we just left. And Kluge is stalking us from around the corner.

We're trapped! Like bugs about to be squashed between Daemon and Kluge.

"You and your little toy are dogmeat!" Daemon emphasizes the "T" word again. Then he swivels his launcher toward Dingus and fires. The puke bomb splats into Dingus' face.

Dingus wipes the puke from his eyes. He shakes his hands, but the puke sticks to his fingers. His ears turn red and are on the upside of purple when his whole body heaves in a giant wave of nausea.

"Aww, your baby toy looks like he's gonna be sick!"

Dingus roars so loud, even Rex backs away. I didn't know he could make such a sound. I swipe my arm across my forehead to mask a glance at the traffic. Still no signal to cross.

Daemon had been inching forward and is now only a few feet away. "He looks like he's gonna blow! What's the matter, baby toy? You gonna barf?"

The crowd behind Daemon had lost interest in Rex for this new spectacle. Some of them chant, *Barf! Barf! Barf!* Daemon smiles over his shoulder, inspired by his audience.

A huge, smoke-filled snot bubble grows out of Dingus' nose from beneath the puke. Daemon points and laughs at him. Kluge laughs. The other kids start to laugh, too.

I sneak another peek at the traffic. The signal has changed.

Dingus' body starts to spin. Faster and faster he goes. Daemon laughs so hard he doesn't pay attention to me, so I take a chance.

I dash across the street and hop onto the curb the second traffic starts up again. I snatch my pocket pilot from its loop on my shorts, aim it across the street, and click to turn Dingus off.

Dingus vanishes. The show is over.

Daemon finally notices that I'm across the street. He yells, "Arghh!"

Now the kids are laughing at Daemon. He balls his fist at them and a few kids drop back. But he turns to me, raises that fist and shouts, "Just you wait 'til the Viarbox tournament Nikola Tosin! I'm gonna turn you into a steaming mass of seventh grade pulp – on live television!"

I had started to run home, but stop and turn. The tournament! Daemon must have entered it too. I look across the street at Daemon.

"Yeah, that's right," he shouts so I can hear him above the traffic. "I know you're entered. I'm entered too. And you're gonna regret this day ever happened."

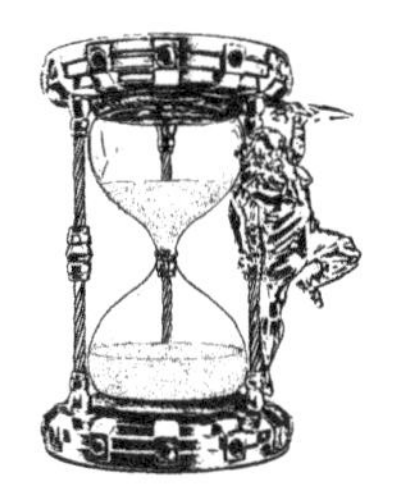

Rex farts and messes everything up

So far today I set a new speed record scrambling up a 200 foot rock wall. No one can climb faster than me, even when the stubbs move from under your foothold. I also won at the Indianapolis Skyway. I jousted, wrestled a crocodile, wing-walked on an old-fashioned biplane and saved the world from an alien invasion. And it's barely past lunch.

Now it's the finals at the 2076 Junior Viarbox tournament. I touch the visual button on my Viarbox earpiece and blink into the next game. Immediately, I feel the cool air in the shade of the massive gnarly trees. I smell pine sap and decaying leaves. An animal roars in the distance and I glance up in the direction of the sound expecting to see Rex crash through the trees. Instead, Nefertiti Naquin blinks in next to me and I jump back, nearly tripping over a tree root. She's tall, dark and at least a year older than me.

"Nik," she says to me with a nod. At least she doesn't laugh.

"Nef," I nod back to her. I reach out and shake her hand in sportsman-like fashion. Then, she turns and sprints deep into the thicket, as if she knows where she's going and already has a strategy planned.

I sprint in the opposite direction, hoping to give her the same impression. I had watched her play the last couple rounds of the tournament. She's good. But, we both made it to the finals.

Daemon is the other finalist. It was down to four of us until Daemon won the demolition derby, completely and unnecessarily destroying the other transport long after the game was decided. Somehow I managed to avoid playing against Daemon up to now. But my luck can't last forever.

I really don't have a strategy. Rex is a brand new game, so no one has ever played it. Nefertiti's strategy is probably just to make me think she has one.

When I hear Rex roar again, I crawl inside a thick cluster of bushes to get my bearings and check out my situation. When you enter a virtual reality game, your clothes adapt to the needs of the game. I look down and see that I'm wearing a camouflage shirt and pants. There is a tool belt around my waist with assorted weapons attached to it. One weapon is a canister-shaped launcher. I assume it's for the little rockets that hang beside it. There is a sturdy armband around my left sleeve with a grooved circle the size of the rocket launcher base. That must be where it attaches.

I shift my weight to more comfortably watch the surrounding forest while I plan what to do next. That's when something shiny catches my eye. It's sticking out of the dirt right beside me.

A game tool! What luck to find one so early in the game! I scrape around the dirt with my fingers and pry it up. It's a whistle on a string.

A whistle? If I blow it, it might help me to find Rex. But it would also help Nefertiti to find me. I hang the string around my neck, but I don't expect to use it. Still, I know better than to throw away a game tool.

Wait! I see another gleam of metal. It's gold and shiny. Something else is buried in the dirt just beneath where I dug up the whistle. I scoop the dirt around it and try to pry it up. It's larger and I have to work at it. It comes loose and I'm able to pull it out.

I brush dirt off and see that it's a fancy little hourglass about four inches long. There are bright jewels embedded into the golden ends and a sort of god-like creature carrying a thunderbolt, snaking his way down one side.

I can't imagine what a fancy hourglass might be used for in a game where all you have to do is kill a tyrannosaur. But I'm confident its purpose will reveal itself. So, I jam the hourglass into my pocket.

Thump! Thump! I feel the tyrannosaur's footsteps getting closer and I settle in under the bush. I smell something awful just before Rex crashes through the trees. The beast looks around and his nostrils flare. I think he can smell me.

To win, I have to take down Rex before Nefertiti does. To make it easier, I can get Rex to eat her and then finish him off at my leisure. But, she might try to get Rex to eat me too, so I'll have to watch my back. Either way, the game doesn't end until Rex is dead.

I had once heard that animals can smell fear. So I close my eyes and breathe slowly in and out. I clench and relax my muscles to make myself as calm as possible. It must be working because Rex wanders off and I'm able to crawl out from under the bush.

The good thing about tyrannosaurs is that they leave really big footprints. So I follow them. The bad thing – at least about this particular tyrannosaur – is that his footprints scatter in all directions. I can't tell which are fresh tracks and which are old.

The forest is a deep maze of trees, roots, and shrubbery. I dart from tree to tree in search of both Nefertiti and Rex. Soon, I don't know where I am and I have no idea which way I'm heading. But, I need to find out.

I scan in all directions for signs of movement from either Nefertiti or Rex. While searching, I note any good hiding places, like wide trees and thick shrubs, in case I need it. Then I take a chance and blow the whistle. No sound comes out of it.

Rex roars in the distance.

I blow the whistle again. Still no sound comes from it, but Rex responds.

A dog whistle! I can call Rex to me without alerting Nefertiti to my location. This is a good game tool. When I hear the thunder of Rex approaching, I dive behind a wide tree.

Rex's roar carries the echo of Daemon's voice. "*... a steaming mass of seventh grade pulp*!" It reminds me of what happens next. The winner of this game has to play against Daemon in the final showdown.

But not the loser.

Which would be more embarrassing? Losing in the finals on live television? Or becoming a steaming mass of seventh grade pulp — on live television?

I could accidentally let Rex eat me.

Losing might be an option.

The mere thought of losing the game on purpose calms me. I press my spine against the bark of the knobby tree. I can hear Rex sniffing around on the other side of it. He's close enough that I can smell his awful breath, but far enough away that he doesn't know where I am. If I jump out from behind the tree and pretend to fumble with the rocket launcher, the tournament audience won't know I threw the game.

Then the sound of Rex sniffing is gone. I peer around the tree and see that Rex's attention is on a bush. Had I wandered in a circle? Is my scent still on the same bush I hid under in the beginning of the game?

Just then, I catch a glimpse of movement behind another tree about twenty yards away. I watch and, sure enough, an elbow peeks out and then disappears behind the tree.

"There you are, Nefertiti."

I reach for the rocket launcher on my belt. As quietly as possible, I screw it into the threads on my armband. Each rocket has a symbol on the label. It appears some are smoke bombs and others are explosives. I choose a smoke bomb in case I accidentally kill Rex and get stuck playing against Daemon later. I fasten the smoke bomb to the launcher.

Click.

At the sound, I stiffen and hurry back against the tree.

It's too late.

The tyrannosaur roars. The ground vibrates as he trots over to my tree. I plant my feet and hold my breath just when the stench hits me – like meat that was left to rot in the hot sun for a few weeks. He has to be right there. Right above me on the other side of the tree. The swarm of insects grows thick around me but I resist the urge to swat at them. A huge glob of saliva slides down my shoulder. Rex is sniffing the branch right above my head.

I dare not move. I have not yet made up my mind about throwing the game. My instinct fights against it even as my mind wants desperately to avoid playing Daemon.

Then I hear a loud rumbling noise. I smell something worse than Rex's breath. Worse than any smell Dingus ever conjured.

The giant tyrannosaur farted.

Nefertiti's tree is behind Rex and I hear her retch. Rex hears it too. His massive body stiffens and his head swings toward the sound.

My winning instinct kicks in. I step out from behind the tree. I lift my arm and press the button on the launcher. The canister sails over Rex's shoulder toward the tree where Nefertiti is hiding. Rex jerks his whole body toward the movement of the smoke bomb and chases after it. I have to jump over his tail as it narrowly misses me.

Nefertiti scrambles into position and aims her weapon. But she's not fast enough. The tyrannosaur opens his giant mouth and, with one bite, bears down on her.

What have I done? Rex has eaten my only hope of avoiding Daemon!

I move in slow motion as if someone else has taken over my body. My hand reaches to my belt for an exploding rocket. I attach the rocket to my armband. It makes a clicking sound but I don't care. I raise my arm and aim the rocket. I press the button.

The small rocket makes a smoky arc-shaped vapor trail as it flies toward Rex. It slams into Rex's back and explodes on impact. Bits and pieces of blown-up tyrannosaur rain down on the forest and on me.

Split, splat. Pit, pat. Drip, drop. Then nothing.

I stand alone in the forest. At first it's quiet, but a new noise grows louder. I can hear the cheers from the tournament crowd.

I press the visual button on my earpiece. The forest scene melts away. The crowd is cheering and all eyes are on me. I am near the center of the arena floor wearing my Viarbox earpiece, sensor gloves and the clothes I had worn to the tournament. An official leads Nefertiti to the sidelines where Daemon stands, sneering.

I pat my hip to grab my pocket pilot, but I check myself, remembering where I am. Clicking Dingus to me now will only make this hideous moment worse.

But the action makes me notice something else. That little hourglass I found under the bush is still in my pocket. That's impossible! Game pieces can't leave the game.

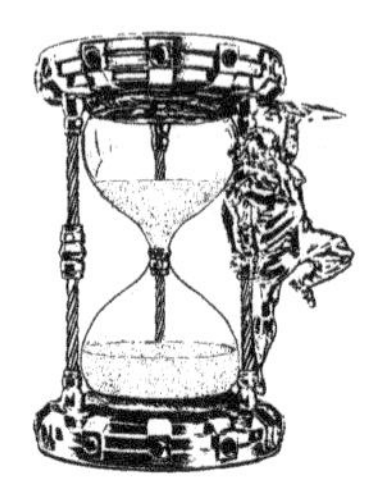

A stupid old-fashioned hologram game

Daemon and I get a one-hour reprieve before the final showdown. It's time for the exhibition, when Viarbox shows off all the new games for the season. This is the whole reason for having the tournament in the first place. A glorified commercial.

I see Daemon strut to the food court with Kluge. So I turn toward the players' lounge.

Dingus catches up with me just outside the door and yanks on my sleeve. "That was the coolest thing I ever saw. Brilliant strategy, bro. Just keep your opponent behind Rex and… Oh man. How'd you come up with it?"

"Huh?" My mind is whirling between Daemon and the hourglass.

"The game! *Rex*. It just went on sale when your game ended. Oh man, that is the coolest. You actually got to control the release of a game. You're part of history! Can I download it? Can I? PuhLEASE?"

"Oh, uh… sure."

Dingus closes his eyes. His ears turn red. Then he opens his eyes wide and smiles. "Got it! Oh man, I can't wait to play. I'll transfer it to your compad as soon as the tournament..." Dingus deflates. "What's wrong, bro? They're getting ready for the exhibition. Let's go watch."

"There you are, Nik!" I turn and see my recent opponent approaching.

"Aww!" Dingus whines. "What are you doing here?"

I give Dingus a quelling eye, then turn to her. "Hi Nefertiti."

"I just wanted to congratulate you."

"Thanks," I say without enthusiasm.

Nefertiti picks up my mood. "Don't pay any attention to Daemon. He's just trying to psyche you out. He's doing it to everyone."

"Yeah, but everyone else didn't get on his bad side," I mutter, remembering the scene from yesterday.

"What you need is a good distraction." She puts her hand on my shoulder and Dingus gives a low growl. The kind that a little dog makes when a transport flies past the house. She snatches her hand away instead. "He's not going to bite me is he?"

"No. Cut it out Ding." The growl stops. "Dingus, can game pieces leave a game?" He's a product of Viarbox and knows about weird stuff like this.

"What? No. Why?"

I pull the hourglass out of my pocket and hold it up.

"Ooh," Nefertiti reaches to touch it.

Dingus beats her to it and snatches it from me. He turns it over in his hands. "Where'd you get this?"

"I found it under that bush."

"What bush?" He mumbles still looking at the object.

"In the Rex game."

Dingus snaps his head to look at me. "Not possible."

"Really," I say. "It was buried under the dog whistle."

Dingus stares at the hourglass and then at me. Finally, he goes to the corner of the room where I had dumped my backpack when we arrived earlier. This is my first tournament and I didn't know what to expect. So I packed some games and things to do in case we got bored between rounds. So far, I didn't need it.

Dingus brings the backpack to the table. "Did you bring your compad?" Without giving me a chance to answer, he opens the pack, peers inside and smiles. He pulls out the plastic computer pad, unfolds it and lays it on the table. Once opened, tiny hologram icons float up and hover above the compad. Each icon represents a program, function or folder. The VR logo opens the Viarbox app. The raging bonfire is where I send anything to be deleted. The exhausted, tiny, postal worker sorts incoming messages.

One icon looks like a small toolbox. Dingus taps it one time and it grows larger. He reaches deep into his pocket, feels around, and then pulls out a wire with a small rectangular plug on one end and a cylindrical plug on the other. He attaches the rectangle end into a port on the enlarged toolbox. Then he inserts the other end into a port on the hourglass. A white box appears in the air, like a blank sheet of paper.

Then Dingus taps an icon that hovers nearby and a hologram keyboard appears in front of him. He types *search hourglass.* A few lines of code appear in the white box. Dingus reads them and frowns. He flaps his hands at the lines of code and they disappear.

He types again. *Search clock.* Again, a few lines appear, but none seem interesting to Dingus. He brushes them away.

Then he types *search time.* Lines and lines of code appear in several new white boxes.

"Jackpot!" Dingus yells and punches the air. Using his finger, he scrolls through the lines of code with lightning speed. I get dizzy watching him. When he's done, Dingus reaches into the code and drags a single equation into the air.

{Displace = Hourglass + Time}

Once separated, the phrase reforms itself into the image of the golden hourglass, except now it's a tiny hologram icon. When that happens, all of the extraneous white boxes disappear leaving only the first one. Dingus flicks that one away with his fingers and the original icons plus the new hourglass icon remain.

"What is it?" Nefertiti asks.

"Looks like a game. It's called *Displace*."

"*Displace*?" Nefertiti says. "What kind of game is it? And what was it doing inside *Rex*?"

"Yeah?" I echo the question.

"Beats me." Dingus says. "Someone put it there."

"So now what?" Nefertiti says.

Dingus cracks his knuckles in a sickening crunch. "Step aside children and let the master do his work." He wiggles his fingers and then double taps the hovering hourglass. Almost instantly, two digital calendar-clocks appear in front of Dingus. One says *Find*. The other says *Send*. They both display the current date and time: Saturday, July 4, 2076 at 2:26 p.m.

A tiny globe rises out of the compad, growing larger and larger, until it presents itself in front of Dingus. He spins it halfway around and touches the North American continent. The globe morphs into a map of the United States. He touches where we live, near Lake Michigan – Chicago – on the map.

A large, ancient-looking bronze bowl materializes in the air in front of Dingus. It's not elaborately decorated like the hourglass. Instead, it's a simple, crude bowl with dents in it. Nefertiti gets off her chair and goes to Dingus' side of the table. She looks into the bowl and gasps.

I stand up to lean over the bowl, too. Inside, I see a kaleidoscope of misty images that swirl and eventually clear to reveal a bird's eye view of Chicago.

Dingus uses his hand and fingers over the image to adjust the view, swiping to move it right and then left. Spreading his hand to zoom out and closing his fingers to zoom in. Finally, he settles the view over the Viarbox stadium, right where the tournament is taking place. Right where we are at this moment.

The parking lot is crowded with transports. The area around the stadium hums with rides and games at the carnival. Transports zoom back and forth and up and down on the highways beside the stadium. When I try to reach into the bowl, an invisible shield prevents me. "I don't get it." I look to Dingus for an explanation.

Dingus sits back and looks through the icons that still hover over the compad. He taps a floating question mark and *Help Menu* appears and fades away. So he taps it twice. When the help menu opens, he scrolls through it at a speed much too fast for humans.

"I think we have to pick a date and we'll be able to see what was going on at that location and on that date."

"What date?" I ask.

"Any date," Dingus says. "In history, that is. You can't go forward."

"Ooh! Let me pick!" Nefertiti says. "Today is the tercentennial, July 4, 2076. Let's go back exactly three hundred years to the original Fourth of July."

Dingus rolls his eyes, but does as she suggests. He reaches up to the *Find* calendar and flips the first two numbers on the century from 20 to 17. The date now shows July 4, 1776.

All three of us look back into the bowl. When the image comes into focus, I see the edge of a wooded area and a crude hut nearby, but mostly flat land with dirt and grass. "The scene should represent what might have been right here, where this building stood three hundred years ago." Dingus says.

"I think you're in the frontier," Nefertiti says. "Can you move over that way?" She points to the edge of the view in the bowl.

Dingus uses his fingers to move around and zoom in and out on the scene in the bowl. We see Lake Michigan in one direction and wilderness in the other. "Ooh!" he says, finally settling on something of interest. "Looks like there were Native Americans in this area. They must be celebrating the Declaration of Independence."

"No, zettahead." Nefertiti says. "They wouldn't have known about it."

From what I can see in the bowl, it looks more like a small skirmish going on between two tribes. On the edge of the fighting, a warrior on horseback chases down a native kid. He isn't really a kid, but he's probably too young to be fighting. Maybe high school age. The older warrior has a gun. The kid only has a bow and arrows.

The kid kicks his horse's flanks and rides behind a boulder. He turns the horse around and quickly loads his bow. The older warrior raises a long, deadly rifle. Both the gun and the arrow fire at the same time. Nefertiti gasps and I think I do too.

The native kid grabs his shoulder as he falls off his horse. There's no sound, so I can't hear him. But I can see the kid cry out when he lands. The older warrior is also thrown when the arrow pierces the horse's saddle. He gets to his feet and pulls a knife from its sheath. The kid scrambles backward, but his enemy is fast. The older warrior bends over the young native's bloody body and raises his knife. The kid reaches up to defend himself.

"Is this game about observing or can you do something to help?" I ask.

Dingus points to the wounded native with one hand and to the *Send* calendar with the other. He gives one of the year digits on the *Send* calendar a light flick of his finger. It flips two notches. The year changes to 1976.

When I look in the bowl the older warrior and the tree are gone. The wounded native is still on his back, but now he's on black asphalt. He opens his eyes, gasps, and struggles to his feet, holding his shoulder as he gets up.

"Where is he?" Nefertiti asks.

Before Dingus can answer, an old fashioned transport plane flies by in the image, momentarily hiding the native from view. After it passes, the young native is on the ground covering his head. He struggles to get back on his feet.

"Looks like he's at a transport station," I observe.

In the bowl, I see several people huddled a short distance from the native. One man hoists onto his shoulder a big black box with *Chicago News 5* printed on the side. A woman speaks into what I assumed is an antique microphone. Two other men stare with their mouths gaping open.

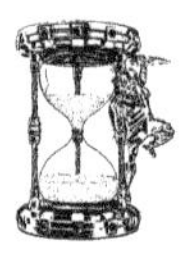

Nefertiti pulls back from the bowl. "Wow. Whoever wrote this game was one weird guy."

I wonder what the point of the game is. "Let's try another," I suggest.

"Oh! Do Philadelphia!" Nefertiti blurts. "That's where all the good stuff was happening in 1776."

"Can I try?" I ask.

"Sure." Dingus says a command to the game and the map reappears.

I point to the southeastern corner of Pennsylvania.

We all look into the bowl.

The scene changes to what must have been colonial Philadelphia.

I use my hands and fingers to zoom around the way Dingus had done earlier. Soon, I see neat rows of little houses lined up on the streets. A crowd gathers outside an important-looking building. The people are dressed funny. Women wear long, puffy dresses and men wear shorts with long socks and triangular hats. Given the date, something big is probably about to happen. Away from the buildings, more people arrive. Some on foot or horseback, others in horse-drawn carriages.

Only one person in the crowd seems like he wants to get out. I see a young boy look over his shoulder as a plump and rather angry-looking man chases him through the crowd.

"There's someone who might need our help," I say. "Check out that kid." I navigate the scene in the bowl to follow him.

The boy emerges from the crowd and runs several blocks, and the man barely keeps up. The boy turns into an alley and ducks into a yard behind a small house. There, he steps behind a barrel and catches his breath for a couple beats. Then he gets up and cups his hand to scoop water from the barrel. He drinks first and then splashes water into his face. When he looks up, the man is right there. The boy kicks him in the shin and the chase is on again.

"Can you help the boy get away?" Nefertiti says.

"He's doing fine on his own," Dingus says.

"Do it, anyway" I say. "I just want to see what happens."

Dingus points to the boy with one hand and reaches up to the *Send* calendar with the other. With a single touch, Dingus sends the boy to July 4, 1976.

We all look back into the bowl. The boy is still in the exact same alley, but it is asphalt instead of dirt. The man chasing him is gone and new people are there. By their clothing, I assume they are people from 1976. The boy's eyes follow the rise of the taller buildings, the rolling transports, and the people – all in quick succession.

I sit back. "So, how do you *play* the game?" I ask Dingus. "How do you win?"

Dingus closes his eyes. I guess he's reading the instructions inside his mind, so I wait. When Dingus opens his eyes, he shrugs. "I'm not sure. The code is harder than anything I've ever seen before. Yet, it looks so simple. I don't understand it. Let's try one more."

I am losing my patience with the game, but it's better than thinking about… what I don't want to think about. I briefly wonder how much time has passed in this one-hour of leisure. This game, however stupid, is turning out to be a good distraction.

Dingus brings up the map again. "How about the other side of the country?" He touches the map at the extreme lower left corner of the country and looks back into the bowl.

The view focuses over water, just beyond a beach. The *Find* calendar is still set to July 4, 1776.

Dingus zooms in and out and around over the vacant expanse of land. "This should be San Diego. I guess no one was there, yet. It's only 1776." Dingus reaches up to the map but I stop him. I see movement along the edge of the view and zoom to settle over it.

It looks like a construction site. A man in a dusty brown robe is pointing and directing while others carry bricks and timbers, or dig trenches. No one seems like they need to be rescued but Dingus points with one hand to the man in the robe, probably a monk or priest I guess, and touches the *Send* calendar with the other.

When I look into the bowl again, I see a white church surrounded by twentieth century highways and buildings. The man in the robe looks as stunned as the boy and the native had.

I pull back from the bowl. "This isn't virtual reality. It's just a stupid, old-fashioned hologram game."

"What's the point?" Nefertiti asks.

"Yeah," I say. "How do you get inside the game?"

Dingus' eyes fly wide open when I say that. He groans.

"What's wrong, Ding?"

Dingus' eyes flick back and forth, from the bowl to the calendar to the Help menu. "What?" I say.

"Oh no," Dingus whispers. "I want to try something," he says a little louder. He returns the view in the bowl to the present day stadium in Chicago. "There's something called a *User* command." He turns his head to the map and says, "Find me."

The bowl switches its image to show the tops of our heads. It's as if a camera is in the ceiling right above us. I look up and waive. "I don't see anything. How can it see us?"

Dingus slaps a hand to his forehead. "I don't think this is a game."

I look down at the hourglass icon and then at Dingus. "It's not a very fun game."

"No," Dingus says. "It isn't a game at all."

"What do you mean? What else could it be?" I look at Nefertiti. She shrugs.

Dingus cups the hovering hourglass icon in his hand and closes his eyes briefly. "There's nothing in the code that talks about points, tools or even goals. It just seems to be about time differential."

I shake my head, not understanding him.

"I don't mean time as in 'what time is it'," Dingus explains. "I mean time as in the date, the year, the century."

"Dingus, just tell me what you're not telling me."

"I think this is a time travel program. *Displace*. That's what it's called, remember? I think we just *displaced* three real live people into a different time."

I shake my head. "You mean, this is real?"

Dingus nods.

"You're joking, right?"

Dingus shakes his head.

Nefertiti gasps. "Oh no! Put them back! Hurry! They have no way to get back to their own time. Put them back!"

"You better put the people back, Ding."

Dingus opens the keyboard and types in the word *replace*. He goes back to the map and bowl and pulls up the image of the airport. The native is no longer on the runway, but a medical transport drives away from the scene. Dingus switches to view the streets of Philadelphia. The boy is gone. In San Diego, I see the white church, but the priest is no longer there.

"I can't put them back unless I can see them and displace them again."

"Where are they?" Nefertiti asks.

"The native must be in the medical transport. The kid and the priest must have gone inside a building." Dingus reads more of the help menu. He types in some code and mumbles to himself. "Let's see... I can set a replacement sequence..." He types some more. "Even in the future, like say... a day, a week, ten days..." Dingus stops typing and shakes his head. "But, that won't work unless they're standing on the same spot of their original displacement. And there's no way to tell them that." He switches the image back to the room where we are at that moment.

I see myself, Nefertiti and Dingus. Then I see a fourth figure in the bowl and gasp. I watch in catatonic horror as Daemon reaches over my shoulder.

"Why don't you join them?" Daemon hisses in my ear. "I'll win the tournament either way. But this way, I get to go home sooner."

In what seems like slow motion, Daemon points three fingers into the bowl just as Dingus had done. And with his other hand he points to the *Send* calendar, which still says July 4, 1976.

Dingus wraps his arms around my backpack. Nefertiti yells, Noooo..."I fall into darkness.

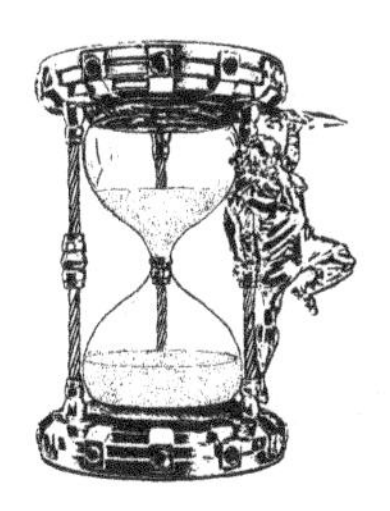

Somewhere below us

I land face down in what feels like a warm, soft tree branch that says, "Ooof" when I hit it. I can see that the trunk of the tree is wearing blue pants. There's a briefcase on the floor beside a pair of shiny black shoes.

Nefertiti is laying on the tiled floor just a few feet away. Her eyes are closed but she moans. Dingus is next to the tree still hugging the backpack. His eyes are open and his fearful expression seems frozen. Like he's made of stone.

The pant-wearing tree barely registers as odd, but I recognize that my virtual friend is in need of a reboot. I reach to grab my pocket pilot from the loop at my waist, point it at Dingus, and click twice.

Dingus disappears, then reappears. He sits up, opens my backpack, and says, "Do you have any snacks in here?"

Two things happen at once. Dingus looks up at me and gasps. And the tree says, "What the…?" and drops me on top of Dingus.

I scramble to get off Dingus, just as Dingus shouts, "Don't move!" He says it so loud that the words echo off the walls as if from a loudspeaker. I freeze. But then I look at Dingus and realize he's not talking to me, but to the tree. I look up.

It's not a tree.

It's a man! A very large man with a shiny brown head, wearing a blue business suit. He looks down at me. I move to stand up and the man starts to take a step to make room for me to do so. But Dingus holds out a hand and shouts, "Don't move!" again in the same loud voice.

The man and I both freeze again.

Dingus turns the backpack upside down and shakes it hard, making all the contents plop, bounce and tumble out. Toys. I hadn't emptied that backpack in a long time. I see all the toys that I had stuffed into that backpack and forgotten over the years, plus the new layer of stuff I had added for the tournament.

Dingus seems interested in only one object and snakes an arm out toward the sticky tape before it can roll out of his reach. He snatches it up and pulls off a piece. Then he leans over and lifts one butt cheek off the floor. I think he's about to fart, but he sticks the tape on the floor beneath him and sits back down.

Dingus rips another piece of tape off the roll and looks up at the man, whose mouth hangs open as he watches Dingus.

"Lift your foot," Dingus commands. The man doesn't move.

"Please," he adds.

The man shakes his head. "Oh! Uh... okay." He lifts one foot and Dingus sticks the piece of tape on the floor under it.

"Thanks," Dingus says to the man, who promptly puts his foot back down.

Dingus stands up. "You can go now," he says. The man doesn't move.

Dingus flicks his chin, motioning for the man to get lost.

The man stays where he is. "Who... Where... What...," he sputters.

"Where are we?" Nefertiti sits up.

"Mark your spot before you move." Dingus tosses the roll of tape to her. "If my theory is correct... and it is," he continues, speaking to me as if Nefertiti hadn't spoken, "We're exactly where we were before." He squints up at the ceiling as if inspecting it. "Well maybe just below where we were. The question isn't where, but when."

"When?" I ask.

"When?" Nefertiti says.

"When?" the man echoes.

Dingus glares at the man. "No, really. You can leave now. Go! Shoo!" He raises his eyebrows at me to do something.

"Oh!" I say. I turn to the man. "Er, thank you for catching me. We, uh, fell and... Er, thank you."

The man looks up at the ceiling and back to me. He shakes his head. "Where did you come from?"

I don't know how to answer to his question, but I do know that Dingus won't explain anything as long as the man is in earshot. "We're fine. Thanks a lot. Um... we'll just be going, now." I bend and start stuffing toys into the backpack.

The man stoops as if to help, but Dingus glares at him and he stands back up.

"Please, Mister." I say. "We're okay. We just need to be alone right now."

"Oh. Sorry." The man frowns, but he picks up his briefcase. With one last look, he shakes his head slowly from side to side. "Far out," he mutters as he walks away.

"You didn't bring any food?" Dingus looks up from the pile on the floor, lower lip sticking out.

"That's your concern just now?" Nefertiti says as she helps stuff items into the pack.

I roll my eyes. Ever since I downloaded an appetite for Dingus, he blinks in hungry. "What did you mean by 'when'?" I say, getting to the main point.

"Let's see," Dingus says. "Daemon pointed to us in the bowl and then to the Send calendar. The date was still on July 4, 1976. So that's *when* we are."

Nefertiti gasps.

I shake my head. "Do you mean Daemon *displaced* us?"

Dingus nods. "That's the last thing that happened, yes."

"And we're stuck in the year 1976?"

"Not stuck," Dingus says. "We just chill here for ten days and then we can go back."

"Why ten days?"

"I was messing with the replacement feature when Daemon came into the room. I had just set it for ten days." Dingus reaches deep into his pocket and extracts something in a crushed wrapper. He sniffs it, smiles and tears open the wrapper.

He points the squashed candy bar at me as he talks. "We're not stuck here forever. If you remember, I tried to replace the three colonials, but it didn't work. That's because they moved from their original displacement location. We have to be on the exact spot of our displacement for the replacement sequence to work. That's why I marked our places where we landed with the tape. But," he leans forward and whispers as if it's a conspiracy, "*They* don't know that. *We* do."

Dingus opens his mouth and bites down on the candy bar.

I pull my eyebrows together to work out the meaning.

"*Dey're* schtuck." Dingus clarifies through a mouthful of masticated candy bar. "*We* armen't,"

Nefertiti gasps again, but this time in excitement. "You mean, they're here, too?"

Dingus nods.

"That means we have a chance to find them and tell them how to get back home?"

Dingus shakes his head.

"Why not?" Nefertiti asks.

He swallows before answering. "Because we're in Chicago. They're not."

"One of them is."

"Okay, so we might have time to help one."

"We're talking about people's lives, *virtuboy*!" Nefertiti spits the name at Dingus. "Real human beings! We have to help them."

Dingus looks like he was about to fire off a retort, but I interrupt him. "Wait," I say. "What are you two talking about?"

"We have a chance to help the native, the boy and the priest," Nefertiti says. "We're here in this time. So are they. We have ten days to track them down and tell them what to do to get back to their own time. Then we can come back here to go home, too. We can do that in ten days."

I shake my head again. "Let me get this straight. We are in 1976."

Dingus nods.

"And this place is the same place as the stadium in our time?" I continue.

"Yes. This is an old fashioned transport station. An *aero port*," Nefertiti says. "They used to call it O'Hare. When transports were invented, the old fashioned aero planes went extinct so they tore down the aero port and built the stadium." Nefertiti looks smugly at Dingus.

"It's called an *airport*," Dingus emphasizes the correct pronunciation.

I interrupt to get back to my review of the situation. "And those three people – the native, the boy and the priest – are here, too?"

Dingus nods.

"You set a replacement sequence for ten days. Then Daemon came in and displaced us with them?"

Dingus continues nodding.

"And the replacement sequence will work for us too?"

"It will work for everyone who doesn't belong in this time. But only if they're standing on the right spot at the right time. Miss the spot, or miss the moment, and you'll miss your chance to go home," Dingus says with finality.

My head is swimming. Ten days! The tournament will be long gone in ten days. I won't have to finish the final round. I won't have to face Daemon. My life will be spared. How bad could 1976 be? I can deal with ten days in an easier time.

"This is perfect!" I say. "I'll miss the rest of the tournament, and we can help the other people while we're here."

Dingus shakes his head. "You won't miss the tournament, Nikola. The replacement sequence will return us to the exact moment of our displacement. When you go back, it will be to the same place and time that we left."

"Will Daemon be there?"

Dingus nods.

"And I'll have to play him in the tournament anyway?"

Dingus shrugs and puts a hand on my shoulder. "Sorry buddy, but yeah."

I groan. Ten days from now, my humiliation – or my death – could be long over. Instead, I now had ten *more* days to worry about it. Unless I end up stuck in this time. That would solve everything.

"In the meantime," Nefertiti says, "we can find those people and help them go home, too!"

"And if we miss the mark? If we miss the moment?" Dingus says. "Then we're stuck here, too. We shouldn't take that risk."

"Yes, we should!" Nefertiti shouts.

"No, we shouldn't!" Dingus counters.

I think about it. I can spend the next ten days helping the native, the boy and the priest. Finding three displaced people can't be any harder than playing Viarbox. I beat every Viarbox game I ever played. I just took down a full grown tyrannosaur for Pete's sake! I can do this with my eyes closed!

And if I get stuck in 1976 forever, how bad could that be?

"I'm in!" I shout over Dingus' and Nefertiti's argument.

"You're what?" They say in unison, turning toward me.

"Let's do it," I say. "Let's help the native, the boy and the priest. We can do this. It'll be like playing a Viarbox game. We've done that before. Dingus, haven't you and I played marathon games that lasted days at a time?"

"But this isn't a game," Dingus says. "You can't turn it off when it's time for lunch or to go to bed. This time it isn't virtual. It's reality!"

"Like you would know the difference, Technoid." Nefertiti says.

Dingus glares at her. "I do know the difference. Better than you!" He looks at me. "Why are you siding with her?"

"I'm not siding with anyone. I'm siding with the right thing to do. We should at least try to help those people."

"What if you get stuck here? Forever!"

I shrug. "So what?"

Dingus stares at me. "Oh, I get it. This is about Daemon, isn't it?"

"No!" I lie.

Dingus looks to the ground for a moment, considering. Finally, he takes a deep breath, and looks at me. "Right. If you're in, then I have no choice." He points a finger at me. "But you're going to make it back. We're all going to make it back!"

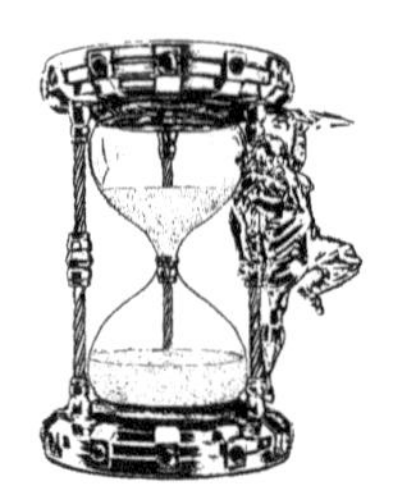

The curious toymaker makes a deal

We follow the maze of corridors until we enter a wide open space. Hundreds of people stand around conveyer belts watching suitcases go past them. Occasionally, someone grabs one and steps away. A new flood of people joins the fray. It's a shifting, slithering crowd and everyone in it seems to have a purpose. Everyone except us.

I flick my head, indicating for Dingus and Nefertiti to meet me over by the far wall.

"We should make a plan," I say to Dingus, who nods in response. "What time is it?"

Dingus blinks once and answers. "Three ten."

"What time were we… you know… displaced?"

Dingus blinks again. "Two forty seven."

Before I can speak, Nefertiti says, "It's July fourth. If we have ten days, then we need to be back here at the *aero port* on July fourteen. Let's try to get here early —by two o'clock if we can. Noon would be better. Just to be safe."

I nod. Any kid well skilled in beat-the-clock games knows it's best to get right down to business. I'm happy to know Nefertiti is one of them. "What day of the week is it, Dingus?"

"Today is Sunday. The fourteenth is a Wednesday."

I tuck that information away in a corner of my brain. "Okay. We're in Chicago. We should try to find the native first. He was wounded and a *medi-port* was leaving the scene when we last looked in the bowl. So he's probably at the *medi-center* right now." I try to form a plan around that information. "But, we don't know how to get to the medi-center or what kind of transportation we can use. The first thing to do in a game is to see what tools you have."

"We have no tools," Nefertiti says. "And, this isn't a game."

"We have what's in the pack." I thump the backpack that's hanging from my shoulder. "We have whatever Dingus has in his pockets."

Dingus raises an eyebrow at Nefertiti. Nefertiti takes a small step backward.

"And we have whatever is available to us in this world," I hold my arms out to embrace the possible tools the wide world might provide. "We need to assess the situation first. And always be on the lookout for new tools."

Nefertiti gives me half a nod and I take it as a half-hearted agreement.

"Good," I nod back. "We know where we are – the *aero port.*"

"Airport," Dingus corrects.

"O'Hare," Nefertiti supplies.

"And we need to get to the medi-center. But we don't know where that is." I look around the big wide room. There's an information desk on the other side of the room. "We can find out over there."

I approach the counter and clear my throat. The woman looks up from whatever she was reading. Then she looks down and leans forward, finally making eye contact with me. She looks around, pausing briefly on Nefertiti, and then faces me again. I rise up on my toes to make myself appear taller.

"Hi. Can you tell us how to get to the medi-center from here?"

The woman looks like she doesn't understand me.

"Where they take people who are hurt," Nefertiti clarifies.

"The hospital?" The woman says. She leans further over the counter and inspects my appearance. Satisfied, she does the same to Dingus and Nefertiti. She turns back to me. "Who's hurt? Is someone sick?"

"No, no." I say. "We want to visit a friend who is hurt. But we don't know how to get to the hospital from here. Can you tell us?"

"Where are your… parents?" the woman asks.

I open my mouth to answer but I don't know what to say. Dingus steps in front of me. "Just over there," he says, pointing vaguely behind us. "Mom's with the luggage and asked us to find out." He could have been talking about anyone in the room.

"Ah," the woman nods. "Do you know which hospital?"

"Which hospital?" I say.

"There are several hospitals in Chicago. Which one is your friend in?"

"Oh!" I say.

Nefertiti yanks my sleeve and pulls me back away from the counter. "We'll just go find out." We retreat to the other side of the room.

"Several hospitals?" I say to no one in particular. This is going to make it hard to find the native.

"Do they have public transports in this time?" Dingus asks.

"I don't know," I say. "Why? What are you thinking?"

"We could tell the driver to take us to the nearest hospital. If that's not the right one, we get in another transport and do the same thing, until we find him."

I can't think of an argument. I look at Nefertiti. She shrugs. Dingus leads the way to the nearest exit.

The heat of the day and noxious transport fumes hit me as we exit the building. Yellow transports line up two rows deep along the curb. I watch a man put luggage into the trunk and the woman hands him a piece of green paper before getting into the transport. I stop.

"Money!" I say. "They still use money in this time. Our personal value accounts won't work."

Nefertiti closes her eyes, looking disappointed. "You're right. I should have thought of that. We learned about money in school. They're called dollars and pence, or something like that."

"It wouldn't hurt to find out how many we'll need," Dingus says. "We might be able to get some."

I approach one of the yellow transports. "Excuse me," I say in my most polite voice. "How many moneys would we need to go from here to the nearest medi… er… hospital?"

The driver looks up and down over my body. "You hurt, man?"

"No, I just want to visit a friend."

"Where are your parents?"

I groan. That's what the lady at the information desk said. "Never mind," I say to the driver.

We back away and move farther up the sidewalk to another public transport. I nudge Nefertiti to do the talking. She's taller and older.

I heard the last word of the driver's response. "Parents." People don't think highly of kids in 1976.

"What time is it?" I ask Dingus.

He groans. "Five minutes past the last time you asked." He turns and leads the way back inside.

Nefertiti and I follow Dingus to a secluded corner of the giant room. It's not well lit, but that will keep prying eyes away from us as we think through our problem.

Dingus opens the backpack and dumps the contents onto the ground. "Maybe we can sell something."

I grimace and glance up at Nefertiti, who's scanning the mess that Dingus has made. I'm embarrassed because there's nothing in the pack except old toys and it makes me feel like a child. Nefertiti pulls her small conferencer out of her pocket, holds it up as if saying *here's my contribution*, and then tosses it on the pile. I'm completely mortified when she starts rummaging through the pile of junk.

Two tiny transports hover over the other toys. She brushes them to the side, revealing an assortment of tools, my old Viarbox earpiece, a few game cartridges, MagnoWand, a pack of nanobot pills, the roll of tape that Dingus used earlier, a flashlight... "What's this?" Nefertiti holds up what looked like a bundle of small snap-together plastic pieces.

"Ooh!" Dingus says. "It's an antique! We can sell that." He speaks with pride at his own brilliance. "They're called *Legos*. I found them in the basement a long time ago."

I take it from Nefertiti and toss it back on the pile. "Dingus... Technoid... it's an antique to us. But not here."

"Oh."

I pick up the yo-yo and throw it out into the large room. It snaps back into my hand. "Junk." I toss the yo-yo back on the pile and lean back against the wall.

At that moment, a shadow blocks the only light that reaches our corner of the room. We all look up in unison.

"Uh... hello again," the large tree-man from earlier looks down at us. "I spotted you coming inside and... there's just something... different about you. I had to satisfy my curiosity."

"You're following us?" I say.

The man shrugs. "Well... I... No... I wouldn't say..." He sighs and points at the Viarbox earpiece that Dingus is holding. "Like that, for instance. It's... different. Mind if I take a look?"

Dingus' mouth gapes open. He drops the earpiece.

"It's okay, children. I own a toy company. *BenCo Toys*. I'm Benny! You know?" He poses as if expecting us to recognize him.

We stare at him.

"Ah, never mind," he say. "That's my problem. No one's ever heard of me. I need a niche. Something new and exciting. Usually, I'm on top of what other companies put out, but I've never seen this stuff before. Can I see them?"

Dingus throws the backpack over the remaining pile, hiding most of the contents from the man's view.

"Who are you?" I ask.

"I just told you," the man says. "I'm Al Bennington. But you can call me Benny." He extends his hand to me. I look at his massive brown hand, then at his face and back to his hand. I put my tiny, freckled hand into his. "Uh… I'm Nikola."

Mr. Bennington shakes my hand with surprising gentleness. "So how did you… you know…" He snaps his fingers. "… like magic. You just… appeared out of thin air. Just like the Indian."

Nefertiti gasps and leans in to me. "The native! They used to call them Indians."

I gasp as well. "The Indian?" I stretch my neck to look up at Mr. Bennington. "You know about him?"

"Yeah, I know about him," Mr. Bennington says. "Everyone knows by now. It's on the news. How did you do it, though? How did you appear from nowhere? Is it magic? Are there more of you coming?"

"No, nothing like that," Dingus says, smoothly. "It must have been a coincidence. A trick of light that made it look like we appeared. We were sitting there for a long time."

"No you weren't," Mr. Bennington says. "I walked down that corridor alone. No one was there. And how do you explain landing in my arms?" He directs his last question to me.

"It was the light," Dingus repeats. "They're not real bright and…"

"Just like the Indian," Mr. Bennington mutters. "You can't deny that. It was caught on film. There was a news crew on the scene and everyone was watching. The Indian just blinked on the scene." Mr. Bennington snaps his fingers again to demonstrate. "Where did you come from?"

I ignore his question for one of my own. "Do you know where the native... er... Indian is right now?"

"It looked like he was shot or stabbed or something. They took him to Cook County Hospital." Mr. Bennington stoops as if to sit, but stops midflight. "Do you mind if I sit with you?"

I gesture to the floor. The man lowers his large frame, crossing his legs the same way as me.

"I bet he's terrified." Nefertiti says. "They'll have to treat him for shock as well as his wounds. At least we know where he is."

Mr. Bennington studies Nefertiti. "You *do* know about him, don't you? You came here the same way he did. But, how? And from where?"

"What..." I begin, not sure how to phrase his question. "Why do you want to know?"

"Me?" Mr. Bennington shrugs. "I'm just as curious as the next guy. Are there more of you coming?"

"No," I say, but then I silently scold myself for answering. "We're not important, really. Forget you saw us. We'll be gone soon."

Nefertiti leans in and whispers. "Maybe he can help us, Nik. You know... pretend he's our parent or something."

I'm not sure what to think. We probably shouldn't risk changing history, and the fewer people involved the better as far as I'm concerned. "No," I whisper back.

"I'd like to help you," Mr. Bennington says.

"No," I say louder. "That's not a good idea."

"I can take you to the hospital." He dangles the words like a candy bar to Dingus. "I can speak for you. I can ask questions. He'll be heavily guarded, you know. The Indian. They won't let you near him."

My head snaps up. That's not a good thing. How can we get a message in if we can't even see him? How can we tell him what he needs to do to go home?

"What do you want from us?" I ask Mr. Bennington. "We have no money. We can't pay you."

"I don't want anything, I swear." He holds up his hands. "I'm not some deranged person, if that's what you're thinking. I just saw what happened. I knew it was just like the Indian." He lifts one shoulder. "You could let me take a peek at your toys, if it makes you feel like a form of payment. I really am a toy maker. Are you sure you don't recognize me?" He poses again, but his portrait-like smile soon fades. "No. I guess you don't."

Nefertiti, Dingus and I look at each other. Nefertiti speaks up. "Mr. Bennington..."

"Call me Benny. I want all children to know me as Benny."

"Benny," Nefertiti continues. "Can I see some form of identification?"

"What? Oh! Uh, sure." Benny reaches into his pocket and pulls out his wallet. He opens it wide and I can see lots of moneys lined up in a neat stack and tucked into a long pocket. Benny pulls three small cards out of the wallet and hands them to Nefertiti.

"That one's my driver's license," he says, leaning over her shoulder. "And that one's my business card."

Nefertiti inspects the card and holds it up for me to see. "*BenCo Toys*. Just like he said."

Benny points to the third card. "That's my pilot's license."

"Pilot's license?" I ask.

"Yeah. I have a small plane."

Ding, ding, ding! The bell in my head rings nearly out loud. A plane! An important game tool. That could help us get to Philadelphia and San Diego! I snatch the two licenses out of Nefertiti's hand and read them. *Albert Bennington.* He was telling the truth about his name. He does know about the Indian. And he did witness our displacement, despite Dingus' attempts to confuse him. It might be smart to keep him close so he can't go blabbing about what he saw to others.

This man just might be useful to us. Without taking my eyes off Benny, I reach out, pull the backpack off the pile of toys and nod in invitation.

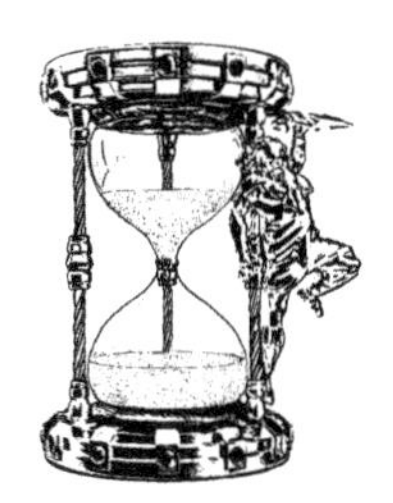

Accomplice to an assassination attempt

Benny looks down at the toys and his face lights up like he is presented with a Viarbox trophy. "Far out," he mutters.

"No," I whisper. "They're right here."

He leans down for a closer look and nudges the toy transports away from the pile. "What's holding them up?"

"They're transports." I lift a shoulder. "They just… hover."

"But, how?" Benny picks one up and turns it over in his hand. "*Hot Wheels*," he says. "I should have known." He tosses it back on the pile where it rests above the mirror. He picks up a hard plastic ball. "What's this?"

Dingus takes it from him. "It's called a *yo-yo*." He throws it toward the large room and it snaps back into his hand.

"There's no string," Benny says, more a question than a statement.

"String?" I look at Dingus. Dingus shrugs.

"A cordless yo-yo," Benny murmurs. He picks it up and throws it. The ball comes back but flies past his head and bounces off the wall behind him. Dingus snakes out an arm and catches it on the return. "Genius," Benny says. He inspects a few more of the items.

Peering at his own reflection in the mirror, Benny narrows his eyes in question to me. I reach out and press the button on the side to switch the reflection to the back of Benny's bald head. His mouth opens, closes, and opens again. He reaches back and touches his head.

I explain the Viarbox earpiece and cartridges and a few other items when Benny asks about them. "Where did you get this stuff?" he finally asks. "I've never seen anything like it. And I'm in the business!"

I look to the others for permission. Dingus shrugs. Nefertiti nods. I turn back to Benny. "Mr. Bennington... Benny... These things haven't been invented yet."

Benny chuckles. "You're playing with me, right?"

"No. Honest!"

"How do you have them if they haven't been invented yet?"

"Tell him," Nefertiti urges.

Dingus nods.

I take a deep breath. "We are from the future."

"Ah, I see." Benny's mouth turns up into a playful smile. "From which planet do you hail?"

"We're from the future, not another planet!" I pick up the toy transport and shake it at him. "Look again. You said yourself that you've never seen these toys before. No one has. Not in this time."

Benny returns his attention to the pile, still smiling. He reads the package for the nanobot pills. After carefully placing it to the side of the pile, he picks up the flashlight. "What's so special about this?" he asks.

"It's called a flashlight. It lets you see in the dark," Dingus says.

"No batteries!" I say. My grandpa used to complain about everything being disposable back in his day. "It's perpetual. It'll last forever."

"Show him Dingus," Nefertiti says to me. She turns to Benny. "Dingus is a... well, he's a..."

"Icksnay on the oytay," I hiss at her. I say to Dingus, "Can you show Mr. Bennington a trick?"

Dingus squints at the ceiling, thoughtful, before turning to Benny. "What do you have in your pocket?"

Benny pulls out his keys and wallet. "This is it."

"Hold them in your hand," Dingus says.

Benny looks from me to Nefertiti and back to Dingus. "You're not going to swipe them, are you?"

"Trust him," Nefertiti says. "This is cool."

Benny holds the items on his open palm. Dingus touches them and pulls away virtual copies of the same wallet and keys. Benny's jaw hangs open. "How'd you do that?"

"Dingus is a..." I fumble. "He made a virtual copy of the items. He can duplicate anything he touches because..."

Dingus lets me off the hook. "I'm a virtual friend. From Viarbox! I'm not a real human. Nikola got me for his tenth birthday."

"Virtual? You mean you're a..."

"Don't say it!" I shout.

"... toy?" Benny finishes.

Dingus' ears change colors at an alarming rate. "Shh, buddy." I say patting his shoulder. "Remember where he comes from. He doesn't know any better. This is the whole reason we wanted to show him. Be still, okay?"

The red in Dingus' ears fades to their usual pink.

I look up at Benny. "He's not a toy. He's my friend. He just happens to be virtual."

Benny reaches out a finger and pokes Dingus' arm.

"Ow!" Dingus says.

"You feel real to me."

"I'm virtual, not a hologram." Dingus rubs his arm.

I grab my pocket pilot. "Should I show him more, Dingus?" When Dingus nods, I click once and Dingus vanishes.

Benny is on his feet in a second – an impressive act for a man of his size and bulk. He feels around in the air where Dingus had been. "Where'd he go?"

"I turned him off," I say.

"Now bring him back," Nefertiti says.

I click the pocket pilot again and Dingus reappears. "Got anything to eat?" I slap him on the back.

Benny's mouth gapes open as he studies Dingus. He reaches out with both hands and clasps Dingus' shoulders. Giving a squeeze, he lets go. Then he bends over and picks up the Viarbox cartridge. "Copyright 2075," he mumbles, reading the label. He turns over one of the Hot Wheels transports. "2071. Incredible!"

"If you help us, I'll let you keep all of this," I say.

"What? You mean it?" Benny says.

"If you'll help us talk to the native. And then… there are two more people we need to find."

"I knew it! There are more, aren't' there?" Benny says. "Oh man. I wouldn't miss this for all the toys in the world."

Benny buys a pack of peanut butter crackers from a machine and hands it to Dingus. Dingus makes a virtual copy and hands me the original, which I stuff into my backpack. Dingus tears into his crackers while Benny leads us to the place where they keep private transports. It's hard to have a conversation with Benny because he's so tall. But I explain along the way why we need a plane for transportation.

"These others are from your time?"

"Not from our time," I say. "We – Dingus, Nefertiti and I – are from a hundred years in the future. The native, the boy and the priest are from two hundred years in the past."

"Far out," Benny murmurs without breaking his stride.

I nod. I guess that really is far out. "None of us can get back to our rightful times unless we're standing on the same spot when we first arrived. But they don't know it. That's why we have to find them. So we can tell them how to get home."

"That's going to be tough with the Indian in lock-up."

"We have ten days to try." I have to look away from Benny to rest my neck. So I talk to his belly instead. "We have to be on our own spot, right here in Chicago, at the same time. It all has to be synchronized."

Benny holds a door open for us. The sudden warmth of the sun hits me and I have to squint at the brightness. I wonder if it's okay to be outside without any UV protection. Our small group walks across the asphalt to a large building with lots of small planes parked around it.

"Here's my plane," Benny says, pointing to an unimpressive yellow Cessna.

Not the fastest thing in the world, but better than nothing. "It'll do," I say. "Does it need fuel?"

"I just flew in, so yes."

"Can you get it ready now? As soon as we deliver the message to the native, we'll need to be on our way to the next stop." Benny didn't move.

I raise my head and shield my eyes with my hand. "Like, right now?"

"Oh! Yeah. Sure. I'll be right back." Benny leaves the three of us and goes inside the hangar.

After he has his plane fueled, we go to the "blue line." That's the train system that connects right to the airport. Benny pays for each of us to get on.

We squeeze onto the crowded train that will take us all the way from the airport to the Medical District. I have to stand and hold onto the pole for part of the way. I'm surrounded by people of this time and I wrinkled my nose at the strong odors. People in this time seem to bury bad smells under worse perfume.

I'm not used to a slow moving world and this ride is ridiculous. To distract myself, I check out the different parts of the ancient city where I live in the future. It seems gray and dirty as we ride past the back sides of people's homes. The train goes through the downtown area and I recognize some of the buildings that are – will be – still in existence in my time. Of course the newer buildings of my time will one day dwarf them. After we leave the downtown area the buildings become shorter again and I can see the sky. It seems eerily quiet with no traffic overhead besides the few airplanes coming and going at the airport.

Benny motions to us when it's time to get off the train. We exit onto a raised platform and Benny points to a building across the busy highway. It's a sprawling concrete castle-like building with the words *Cook County Hospital* printed across the blue overhang to the main entrance. Hundreds of windows are nested between neat rows of columns built right into the face of the building. The only things missing are gargoyles. There's a crowd gathered at the entrance facing a woman at a podium.

I follow Benny down the steps to street level and across the bridge that spans above the highway traffic. I cough at the black cloud of fumes that rise up from the transports.

We reach the hospital. I stand at the back of the crowd and can't see anything. The woman wraps up her speech. "That's all I have to report about John Doe. If anyone has information that can help the investigation, please contact the hospital."

When she's done talking, people shout questions.

"How was he wounded?"

"What's his real name?"

"Has his family been contacted?"

"When will he be released?"

The woman says, "I can't answer questions. I've told you everything I'm permitted to tell you. That's it." She taps a couple pages on the podium and turns toward the entrance.

I must get to the front of the crowd. I duck down and crawl through the forest of leg. "Excuse me!" I jump up and waive my arms. "Excuse me!" The woman steps through the open door without a backward glance.

A man in a black suit steps up to the podium. "That's it folks. There's nothing more. No one but family gets in to see him. No exceptions. I'm sure there's more important news to report elsewhere." He turns and follows the woman's path into the building. Two security guards flank the main entrance to the hospital.

When I try to pass, the guards step in front of me, arms folded. One of them says, "Go home, kid."

"I have to get in."

"No one gets in."

"But… This is a med… a hospital. It's a public place isn't it?" I'm actually not sure. Medi centers are public places in my time. Maybe they're not in this time.

"Too bad. Go home."

Instead, I duck between the two guards and scurry into the hospital lobby.

"Hey! Get back here!" The security guards chase after me and one grabs me by the collar.

"Lemme go!" I shout. I kick his leg. The man yowls, but doesn't let go.

I see Benny muscle his way through the crowd. He points toward me but I can't hear what he says. Surprisingly, the guards let him pass. Nefertiti and Dingus step through the doors behind him.

"Here. Here." Benny says, rushing up to the man who's holding my shirt. "Let the boy go. He's with me."

The man lets go and gestures with his chin at the door. "All of you need to leave."

"We need to see the native," I say.

"Why?" The man braces his feet at shoulder width and crosses his arms. With his dark sunglasses and black suit, he looks like one of those agents at the White House protecting everything behind him, which at the moment is a row of empty chairs. He eyeballs us like he's scanning us for weapons or something. I hope Dingus isn't carrying anything he shouldn't.

Benny puts a hand on my shoulder and squeezes. I take that to mean I should be quiet and let him do the talking.

"We're not reporters," Benny says. "But we need to see the Indian. It's important. Are you in charge?"

"I'm Special Agent Archibald Pheloni, FBI," the man says. "And you are?"

Benny leans way back and stretches out his hand. "I'm Al Bennin…"

"I need to see your ID." Special Agent Pheloni says, without accepting Benny's hand.

"Yeah, sure." Benny retracts his hand and gets out his wallet. He hands one of his licenses to the agent.

Agent Pheloni reads the name aloud. "Albert Bennington."

"Perhaps you recognize me?"

The agent peers at his face and raises an eyebrow. "Should I?"

"He's Benny!" I say. "From BenCo Toys."

The man seems unimpressed. "How do you know the pris… uh, patient?" he says.

"Well, can you first tell me why we can't see him?" Benny asks.

"Tell me his name."

"Running Bear," Dingus blurts. I have no idea where that came from, but I'm glad Dingus has a quick mind. If the hospital staff is still calling him John Doe, then they don't know his real name either.

Pheloni narrows his eyes at Dingus before looking back to Benny. "Why do you want to see him?" he demands.

Beads of sweat appear on Benny's forehead. "We have a message for him."

"Give me the message. I'll see he gets it."

"Oh! Yeah, sure. We just have to tell him…"

I kick Benny softly in the shin. "We have to deliver the message personally," I say.

"I can't let you do that."

"Why not?" Benny says. "Why all the security?" He gestures to the guards outside the doors.

"He's being held for questioning. No one gets in to see him."

"Questioning? What for?"

Pheloni rolls his eyes. "Why do you think? Today's the bicentennial and we have a lot of important people flying in and out the airport. He was armed. Inside the airport. On the runway, in fact! And he was shot, which means someone else is out there. He could be an accomplice to an assassination attempt."

"That's not why he was on the runway," Nefertiti blurts out, but then Dingus shoots a glare at her and she clamps her lips.

Pheloni watches the exchange. "What do you know about it?"

"Nothing." Benny says. "We just have to deliver a message."

"Do you speak his language?"

Benny takes a handkerchief from his jacket pocket and wipes his forehead. "Language?"

"Yes. Of course you know he doesn't speak English."

"Oh yes. We know that."

"Wait here." Pheloni goes to the Information Desk and picks up the phone.

"Do you think he's buying the story?" I whisper to Benny.

"Not a chance. But give him a breath mint!" Benny waves the air in front of his nose.

Pheloni returns a short time later. "You can see him for a minute. Follow me."

"Yes!" I exchange a behind-the-back, low-five with Dingus. If the other two colonials go as easy as this, we'll be back in Chicago in no time and have a whole week to relax and get to know 1976.

We follow Agent Pheloni down a long corridor that leads to the back of the building. After two turns and two more corridors, we get into an elevator. When it stops on the seventh floor, we step off into a reception area.

"The kids have to wait here. You come with me." Pheloni says to Benny. They go to a set of doors at the back of the room. He motions to a woman behind the window. There's a buzzing sound and Pheloni pulls the door open. He motions for Benny to go first through the doors.

"Now what?" Nefertiti asks. "Benny doesn't know the date or time. He doesn't even speak the same language. There's no way he can deliver the message."

"I guess we wait and see what happens." I sink down into a chair in the reception area. "Maybe they'll let us in next."

"Oh man, I wanted to see the native guy." Dingus thuds into an empty chair beside me.

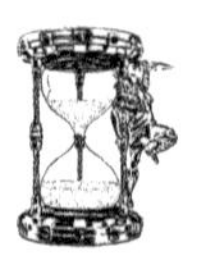

We wait... and wait... and wait. I reposition myself on the furniture a hundred times. Nefertiti paces. I count tiles on the ceiling. The television in the room changes programs for the third time since we arrived. I look out of curiosity, sometimes commenting on the 'old fashioned shows', but mostly I watch the double doors for Benny.

Eventually, the woman behind the window nods farewell to us. She leaves with her purse dangling from her arm. "What time is it?" I ask Dingus for the umpteenth time.

Dingus pulls an old-fashioned wrist watch out of his pocket and hands it to me. "Here. I'm tired of telling you."

"Six o'clock," I observe and fasten the watch to my wrist. "That agent said we could only visit for a minute. They have long minutes in this time."

I am already watching the doors when they finally open. I dig my fingers into the arms of the chair when Pheloni's dark eyes glare at me. Something is wrong. The man strides toward me, his lips in a thin straight line.

I catch a glimpse of Benny behind the agent but another man holds him back. "Nikola, run!" Benny shouts. "Get out of here!" The doors close in front of Benny, trapping him on the other side.

Pheloni lunges toward us and I don't wait to find out what went wrong. "Let's go!" I yell. I jump out of my seat. Dingus grabs the backpack and joins me. Nefertiti follows.

"Stop!" Pheloni works his way through the chairs.

I scale the sofa and head down the hall. Nefertiti pushes a wheelchair back toward the agent. Dingus knocks over a laundry cart to block his path.

We run through the doorway under the Exit sign. It leads to a stairwell, where we skip steps all the way, turning at each landing. Down, down, down we go for all seven floors. I can hear Pheloni's footsteps a couple floors above us. At last, I see the exit at the bottom. The door bangs against the outside wall as we burst through it into the early evening air.

We dive into a nearby dumpster and I close the lid a mere second before I hear the exit door slam open again.

I'm gasping for breath, but I dare not move or make a sound. I'm able to peek out from a small rust hole. Pheloni looks up and down the alley behind the hospital. He runs around the side of the building. A minute later he returns. "You'll be back!" he shouts into the air. Then he talks with certainty and it gives me the chills. "I have your little time traveling friend. You'll be back." He yanks open the door and it bangs one more time against the wall as he steps back inside.

"Stay down and be quiet," I whisper in the dark.

"Ewww. What's that smell?" Nefertiti says.

Dingus answers. "That's your breath blowing back in your face."

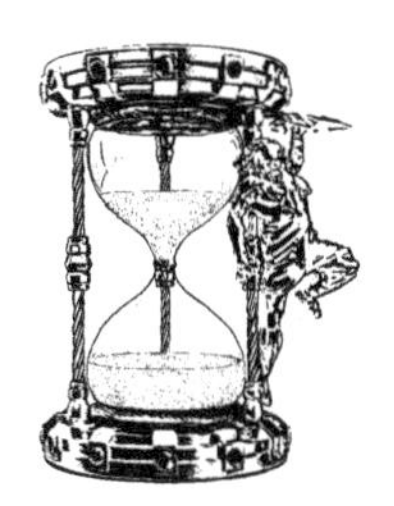

Virtually a plan that could work – maybe

We wait in the dumpster until I'm confident Pheloni isn't coming back.

"Is he gone?" Nefertiti whispers.

"Yeah." I climb out and sling the backpack over my shoulder. But, just in case he's not, we dash around the corner, away from the hospital, and run several blocks until Dingus is out of breath and begs us to stop.

"Any ideas?" I sit on a cement ledge.

"We could stand a good sanitizing," Nefertiti says.

Dingus, still panting, looks like he's about to make a wise crack, but he stops and snifs his armpit. "Yeah, we could."

I look at the old-time watch that's now secured on my wrist. Then I get out my pocket pilot and click to refresh Dingus.

Dingus inspects his clean hands. "That takes care of me. What about Stinky?" He gives Nefertiti a nudge. She elbows him back.

Across the street, I see a sign blinking 'Vacancy' on the decrepit building and a poster in the window says in black print, "$40." Next door to it, another sign blinks 'Pizza.'

"Hey, Dingus, are you hungry?" I just refreshed him, so I expect his nod. "Look across the street." I point to the two signs. "Food and a place to clean up and figure out what to do next."

"We don't have any money," Nefertiti reminds us.

"Yes we do." Dingus reaches in his pocket and pulls out the virtual copy of Benny's wallet.

Nefertiti raises an eyebrow. "Can we use that?"

"Why not?" Dingus hands the wallet to me. "It'll work as long as I'm in range. Then the money will simply disappear."

"But, that's stealing!"

"It's a game tool."

"This isn't a game!"

I open the wallet and pull out the wad of cash. It feels real to me, just like Dingus. It's illegal to make virtual replicas of anything valuable in our time. No one is fooled anyway because everyone owns a scanner to tell the difference. Besides, we use personal value accounts instead of paper money. PVAs are virtual. Real cash has no value other than what a collector might pay for it in our time.

But, we're not in our own time.

I shrug. "Let's see… six twenties, some tens… fives… ones… We can get a room for forty." I point again to the sign across the street. "I hope the food doesn't cost more than that. C'mon."

We go across the street to the hotel. A man behind a glass window is reading a newspaper. He doesn't look up but he says, "What do you want?"

"We'd like a room, please," I say.

"You got money?" the man says, still not looking up.

I hold up the wad.

"It's forty bucks for the night, plus a ten dollar deposit." The man looks up from his paper. "You got fifty bucks?"

I pull two twenties and a ten out of the wallet, hoping they mean "bucks" and pass them through the little hole at the bottom of the glass.

The man passes a key out to me. "Up the steps. Third door on the right. Check out by ten. You'll get the deposit back when you turn in the key."

"Don't you need to know our names?"

"Why? You someone important?" He laughs and looks away.

"At least he didn't ask for our parents," Nefertiti says. We go next door for pizza before heading up to our room.

Once upstairs, I use the sanitation room first. When I come out, Nefertiti and Dingus are already eating. I take Nefertiti's spot on the bed while she takes her turn to sanitize.

"This tastes funny." Cheese drips from Dingus' chin. I shrug and pick up a slice.

A half hour later, Nefertiti emerges wrapped in a towel with her hair dripping onto her shoulders. She puts two wire hangers containing her clothes in the closet. Then she opens each of the dresser drawers, finds an extra blanket and wraps it around herself, over top of the towel. She hops up on the bed beside me.

"Gee, Nef…" Dingus starts but she puts up a hand to stop him. "You keep your distance, Technoid!"

I clear my throat. "We need a plan." I say, bringing the meeting to order. "We have to figure out what to do next. I think we should head to Philadelphia. We have a schedule to keep and we have to come back to Chicago at the end of the ten days so we can be on our marks when the replacement sequence runs."

"Yeah," Dingus agrees.

"No!" Nefertiti jumps in. "We have to rescue Benny. We can't leave him there."

"We can get Benny when we get the native," I say. "We have to come back anyway, right?"

"Yes, but he was going to help us." Nefertiti starts. "We need him."

"We'll have to figure out a way to move on without him." I don't allow room for argument. "Try to think of a way to get to

Philadelphia from here." I dump the contents of the backpack on the bed between us. "These are our game tools."

"This is *not* a game," Nefertiti says.

I ignore her. "We'll collect more as we go along, but right now, this is all we have. Think like you're playing Viarbox. But remember, we're in this time and not our own."

We each stare at the objects. I pick up Benny's wallet and take everything out of it. I count the money. "A hundred and twenty-one."

"Plus ten when we get the deposit back tomorrow," Nefertiti reminds me.

"A hundred and thirty-one then," I say. "This plastic thing says Master Charge and this one says Diners Club. I think they're some kind of credit plates."

"Benny might not like it if we use them," Nefertiti says. "That would register against his real account."

I nod. "We'll wait and see how desperate we get."

"So that's it?" Nefertiti says. "That's all we have?"

"No. Everything... *anything* in this pack is a potential game tool."

"Except that it's not a game! Besides," Nefertiti picks up the yo-yo and shoves it in my face. "How is this a tool?" She drops it and picks up the Viarbox headpiece and waves it in my face. "Or this! How are these toys going to get us to Philadelphia? Or California? Huh?"

I slap the headpiece away from my face. "Everything has potential. That's the point. We have to try to find a different use for it."

Dingus sits quietly during this exchange. I notice him staring with his own brand of mischief in his smile. "What's up, Ding?"

"Wings of Duke," Dingus mumbles, barely audible.

"What?"

Dingus reaches into the pile and pulls out the virtual copy of Benny's keys. "We don't need Benny. We can fly!"

"Ahhhhhhhhh!" Nefertiti squeals from the backseat as we take to the air in Benny's Cessna. We climb higher and higher and are out of reach in mere moments. Soon we're miles away from immediate danger.

"We did it!" Dingus shouts from the pilot's seat.

"You're flying too low." I say. Dingus almost flies us into some bicentennial fireworks.

"I'm in the kids' lane."

"There is no kids' lane in this time," I say. "Go higher. Get up to the regular lane. You can't look conspicuous."

The Cessna jolts as Dingus takes us higher and he fights to keep control. After he steadies it, he swipes his brow with his forearm.

"I thought you said you could do this, Dingus!" Nefertiti says.

"I'm sorry! I logged a lot of miles into a lot of these old-time planes. I just have to remember which one I'm flying and when."

"Don't make him nervous, Nefertiti." I say. "He's doing fine. You're doing fine, Dingus. Don't be nervous." I pat Dingus' shoulder.

"I can't watch." Nefertiti puts one of the small pillows over her face.

Everyone remains quiet as Dingus operates the plane. "We're going to have to land somewhere remote," I say. "They probably have us on sky-watch."

"Radar."

"Whatever. The point is, I'm sure they can see us. They'll know when and where we land." I peer out the window to search the sky behind us. "I'm surprised no one is tailing us right now."

"Don't bother him, Nik" Nefertiti's muffled voice floats out from behind the pillow.

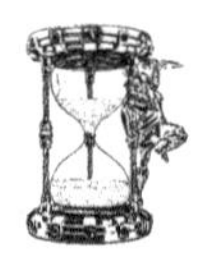

The ride is bumpy and long. At times, I have to remind Dingus to increase his altitude, but since Dingus mostly flies below the main skyways of this time, we don't encounter oncoming traffic. Dingus avoids flying near airports or in other traffic patterns.

"Can you find Philadelphia?" I ask.

Dingus lifts a shoulder. "As long as they didn't move it in the last hundred years." He tilts his head toward the backseat. "Your girlfriend's asleep."

I can hear Nefertiti's rhythmic breathing. She's lucky. It's very late and I've been feeling the pull of sleep too. But I force myself to stay awake for Dingus. "She's not my girlfriend."

"Then why did you let her come?"

"Let her…? I didn't let her! We didn't have a choice."

"You let her hang out with us in the player's room."

"So what? Why do you hate her so much, Ding?"

"Why do you like her so much?"

I don't know how to answer that. She seems nice. But that doesn't make her a girlfriend. Just a girl. "She seems like she wants to be my friend. So what?"

"But, I'm your friend!" Dingus says. "I can do more than she can. She can't tell you when you have to do something. She can't get you out of trouble. And you beat her in the tournament. At least I would have been a better challenger."

"You get me *in* to more trouble than you get me out of! And she did make it to the finals." I smile but he doesn't smile back. "Look Ding. Normal kids have more than one friend. That doesn't mean they stop liking their other friends. At least I don't think that's what happens." I lift a shoulder. Ding has been my only friend for a long time. I'm kind of new at this.

I look out the windshield to think of what he might say, but I see the lights of what must be Philadelphia on the horizon. Oh no! "Dingus, we can't land at the airport. The security and cops will be all over us when we get off the plane."

"Leave it to me," Dingus says.

I trust Dingus completely. The city is bright from our viewpoint. A man speaks to us on the radio. Dingus has been using Benny's call number whenever we come near other airports. He tells the man on the radio that we're off course and 'the pilot' is sick. The man clears us for emergency landing.

Instead of going to the Philadelphia airport, Dingus circles the city to find somewhere else to land. I point to what appears to be a deserted highway with a strip of lights here and there along the edges. "Can you land on that?"

Dingus studies it for a moment. "It doesn't look real wide, but this is a small plane. And there's no traffic."

"It goes smack into the middle of the city," I say. "If we land there, we can follow it the rest of the way on foot."

"What have we got to lose?" Dingus says.

"Our lives!" Nefertiti says, sitting up.

"Who woke her up?" Dingus says.

"Nefertiti, be quiet. Don't make Dingus nervous."

She scrunches her lips together.

Dingus lowers the plane down toward the highway. I see the red lights of a couple of big hauler transports in the distance ahead of us and nothing behind. Dingus takes the opportunity to put the plane down.

"You sure you can do this?" I ask.

"I'm sure."

"Don't do it if you're not sure."

"It's okay. Shut up. I can do this. Don't make me nervous."

Nefertiti jabs me in the ribs, her own mouth still clenched.

Down, down, down, we go. The wheels touch the road, bounce once and then glide on the road surface, nice a smooth. I'm actually impressed with Dingus' landing. Then, I look out the window and see that the wing barely misses over the center guardrail of the highway. "You're over too far!"

"There are poles on this side!"

"Watch out for the sign!" I hold my breath as we passed under a green highway sign.

The plane slows.

"Stop, stop, stop, stop," Nefertiti whispers.

"Stop, you stupid plane. Stop," Dingus mutters.

"Stop!" I shout as the wing is about to hit a pole on my side of the plane.

The wing hits the pole.

The plane jolts and turns sideways. The pole crashes on top of the plane. Nefertiti shrieks. We endure a few moments of twisting metal and a loud crashing noise and, finally, all is quiet and still.

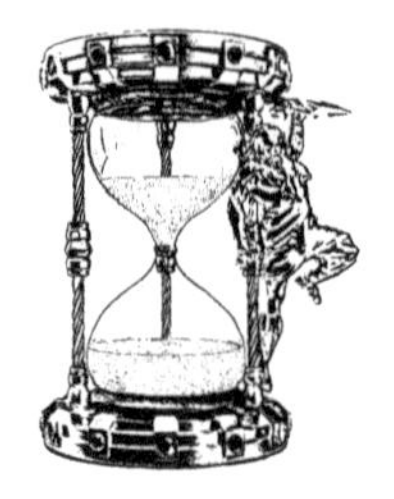

Old City wasn't so old back then

I grab the backpack and, one by one, we jump out of the wrecked plane and run toward the exit ramp of the highway. A police siren wails in the distance, growing louder. I look over my shoulder. "It's okay," I say. "They won't get past the plane." As the words come out of my mouth, a rumbling noise rises up and a helicopter search light appears over the wrecked plane. Luckily we're far enough away not to be caught in the light. "Get under the trees!" I shout. "Keep moving!"

We run up the darkened ramp, staying close to the shaded edge, toward a smaller road. As we run, I watch for hiding places, but nothing looks good. My legs keep moving, not knowing where we're going. Occasionally I glance over my shoulder for the helicopter. It stays hovered with its spotlight over the highway, getting farther away as we continue to run.

"Stop!" Dingus finally yells. "Stop… I gotta… stop."

Nefertiti and I stop with him. Dingus bends over with his hands on his knees, sucking virtual air into his virtual lungs.

Nefertiti looks back. "I don't see anyone. Now what?"

"I don't know," I say. "We should keep moving or duck out of sight somewhere." I walk on and Nefertiti falls into step beside me. I hear Dingus panting, but following.

After what feels like miles later, Dingus finds a pile of large cardboard boxes folded flat next to a dumpster. We are exhausted and I am happy to get a few hours of sleep. We each crawl between layers of boxes, using them like makeshift sleeping bags. I'm asleep before I have time to think what might else be crawling inside them.

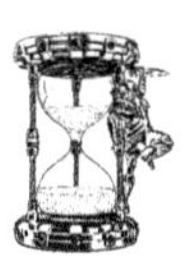

I awaken to the sound of traffic and muted voices. The past twenty-four hours drift into my memory – the tournament, Daemon, the hourglass. Then I remember I'm no longer in the year 2076 and I sit up. Dingus and Nefertiti are already up and scheming something. I make a mental note that it is Monday morning, July 5, 1976.

"What's going on?" I slip out of my box and join the others.

"Nik!" Nefertiti says. "Dingus saw a public transport. It stopped to pick up people. This is a transport route into the city. We can follow the next one or maybe try to get on it. We have plenty of money left…"

"Sounds like you're feeling better." I resign myself to the task ahead. "How often does it stop here?"

"Since the transport just left, I think it'll be some time before the next one."

The sign where the transport stopped has the word SEPTA printed on it. Beyond the sign, I see a golden arch at the other end of the same block. It's archaic, but recognizable as a place to get breakfast. Dingus must be starving by now. I'm pretty hungry, too.

"Good," I say. "Let's get something to eat."

Fifteen minutes later we're sitting on the curb under the transport sign, each with a breakfast sandwich and a small carton of orange juice. We barely finish our breakfast when the transport arrives. The marquee on the front of the transport says 'Market Street.' We board, pay the money, and are finally on our way into the city.

Just like everything else in this time, the transport ride is slow, stopping every block to let people on and off. Most of the time it's so crowded that people have to stand and hold onto poles and balance themselves. I look out the window and count down the numbered streets. We ride the length of Market Street for some time as the numbers get lower and lower. I wonder what happens when the street numbers run out. But then Nefertiti gestures to get off. Dingus and I follow.

"Why'd we get off here?" I ask.

"I saw something I want to check out," Nefertiti says.

We turn the corner and backtrack a block. Nefertiti stops to read a sign in a window. It's about a tour of something called *Old City*. "When the boy was displaced," she explains, "it was from a spot that existed in his time. This is a big city now, but it wasn't so big back then. He would have arrived somewhere in this old part of the city."

"I think we're already here. Look!" Dingus says.

I look up from a poster about Independence Hall and see the same building just a block away. A man and woman stand next to us. "Hey, where'd you get that map?" I ask the man, who is reading one.

"From our hotel lobby," the man says.

"Where's the hotel?"

"Any hotel lobby will have maps. There's one a few blocks down that way."

We practically run all the way. When we get to the lobby I take a map out of the kiosk. I also grab some brochures. Dingus sneaks a newspaper from the counter. Outside, we pause to read the cover article.

Toy Maker's Stolen Plane Ditched in Philadelphia

Eastbound Schuylkill Expressway near the Spring Garden Street exit became a makeshift landing strip for a private plane, owned by Chicago toy maker, Albert Bennington. The plane is believed to have been stolen from O'Hare yesterday. According to sources, the plane's pilot reported the need to make an emergency landing and was cleared to approach, but instead went around the city and landed on the highway. Authorities confirmed an inspection of the plane showed physical damage, presumably caused by the landing. Otherwise, no mechanical problem was evident, although the investigation continues. No one was found on the plane or near the scene.

According to authorities in Chicago, witnesses claim to have seen three children boarding the plane just before it took off from O'Hare last night. It is believed the pilot was already on board. It is not known if the pilot was Mr. Bennington or who the children are.

Mr. Bennington could not be located for comment of either the disappearance or re-appearance of his plane. He was last seen in Chicago when the plane arrived yesterday afternoon. The small craft was removed from the highway during the night, however, ... (cont. pg B7)

See related story on page A3, Recent Mysteries at O'Hare International Airport.

"Oh no!" I fold the newspaper without reading the rest.

"What?" Nefertiti asks.

"The story is in the paper and it's linked to the Chicago incident. It's probably in the Chicago papers, too."

"Which means," Nefertiti picks up the explanation, "That agent will read about it and know where we are."

"If he doesn't know already," Dingus contributes. "Don't forget, he's an FBI agent. He probably has connections."

I nod. "Either way, he knows. We'll have to be careful."

Nefertiti, Dingus and I wander the streets of the old part of the city for several hours looking for any clue that might lead us to the colonial boy. It's much less complicated to cross the streets than it is back home and we have no trouble adapting.

"Let's think logically," Nefertiti says. "The boy would have to find shelter like we do. If we find his shelter, we'll find him."

I'm ashamed I didn't think of that myself. I have to remember to think in game-mode. As it is, Nefertiti is doing it better than me. "So where would he look for shelter?" I ask.

"A hotel!" Dingus answers.

Nefertiti shakes her head. "He wouldn't have any money. Or at least nothing from this time. He'd be stranded. Like a homeless person."

"Maybe they have shelters. You know, so the homeless don't freeze at night," Dingus says.

Nefertiti shifts her eyes skyward, as if praying for patience. "It's July, Dingus. No one is going to freeze at night."

Still… I add homeless shelters to my mental search list along with any other sites where the boy might set up camp. As we walk, I look for anyone who might be him – dressed the way he might dress, talk the way he might talk – any sign at all.

We spend the next couple hours wandering the crowded streets. Dingus breaks a long spell of silence. "I think this town doesn't have any homeless kids."

I've been noticing the same. While there are swarms of tourists, there are no homeless under the age of 'really old.' And they're in plain sight, standing on street corners asking people for money, not in shelters.

"What are we going to do?" Nefertiti asks. "We should think about our own shelter for the night."

"We have all day for that," I say.

"I'm hungry," Dingus says.

I stop and Nefertiti bumps into my back. "Food," I say.

"Yeah, let's eat." Dingus licks his lips.

"No. That's not what I mean," I say. "The boy has to eat, too. What would he eat? He wouldn't have any money, so how would he get food? Where would he go?"

"Let's consider it over lunch."

"Dingus!" Nefertiti says.

"What? I think better on a full stomach."

"That's true." Nefertiti rolls her eyes. "He didn't think of flying the plane until after he had a pizza in him. Maybe if we stuff him with a seven course dinner, he'll get us and everyone home before nightfall and still have time to cure the common cold."

"It's already been cured," Dingus says.

"Figure of speech!"

"Yeah, but old people say it."

"Okay, okay! Let's eat." I stop the banter. "But we have to watch our money. Let's figure out how to get food without spending anything. Maybe that will lead us to the boy."

"That's dumb," Dingus says. "He could just create something in his Nanofood moleculizer."

"For Pete's sake, Nik, feed him."

"Maybe he would go fishing," Dingus mumbles.

I shrug. "Forget lunch. Let's see if this town has a river."

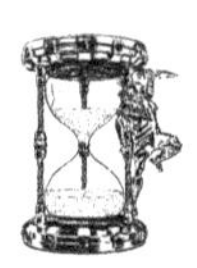

We find a river a few blocks away at a concrete park called Penn's Landing. But, at the waterfront, we can't find anywhere for a kid to get down to the water's edge with a fishing pole. At least, not without suspicious looks from adults.

"What about hunting?" I say.

The three of us turn in unison to face the concrete city.

"The only animals he'd catch here are cats and dogs and maybe a rat or two," Nefertiti says.

"There's a lot of trees. Maybe there are squirrels in the parks," Dingus suggests.

Nefertiti shrugs. "Maybe. Since you're the expert, how would he catch a squirrel?"

"Climb up a tree and act like a nut," Dingus quips.

I roll my eyes.

Nefertiti puts her hands on her hips. "Can we be serious?"

"When my dad wanted to catch a groundhog that tunneled into the greenhouse," I say, "he set a trap. Maybe we can check the park for traps."

Dingus' belly rumbles loud and Nefertiti giggles. I close my eyes, hoping for patience. But my own hunger wins. "The squirrels can wait. Let's get something to eat."

"Good! I'm starving."

"And I'm tired of walking," Nefertiti adds.

We purchase one large Philly cheese steak at the nearest sandwich shop. Dingus makes a copy for himself, and Nefertiti and I split the real one. We feed three for the price of one. When we finish our sandwiches, we spend the rest of the afternoon searching.

But not much finding.

"Maybe we're doing this wrong." I kick a stone that's really a loose chunk of sidewalk. "He could be inside the buildings. You know… site seeing, like a tourist." I look back and forth between Dingus and Nefertiti waiting for agreement. They look at each other, then back to me and shrug in unison.

From our spot on the corner of Third and Arch our options are the Betsy Ross House and the old Quaker Meeting House. The Meeting House wins, since it doesn't cost anything to get inside. First, we circle the large building, which includes lawns, trees, a cemetery and other places a sightseer might go. I also look for anything resembling a squirrel trap, but find nothing.

When we get inside, I realize it has grown late and the building will be closing soon. Fortunately, for such a big building, there's not a lot of places to look. There's a large cafeteria or gymnasium type room to the left, the central lobby, and a theater-like church room to the right. There are more rooms off the lobby, but tourists aren't allowed back there. We go to the right toward the church room.

"Do you think he might sleep in a place like this?" I touch the wooden door frame, which both looks and smells centuries old.

"Hmm, maybe," Dingus agrees. "In fact, we should start thinking about where we're going to sleep tonight."

I look around. "We could stay here." The building is old and certainly cozier than a cardboard box in an alley. If we're going to stay, we need to decide right here and now because it is nearly closing time.

The large church room is something of a square religious stadium. The balconies, benches and pews all face toward the center. I am happy to see cushioned pews. That is, until I sit on one. It is hard and crunchy. They must be as old as the building.

While sitting, I notice a wooden ring nested in the floor boards. I get up and thunk my foot inside the cut-out square that surrounds it. Sure enough, it sounds hollow. It must be a trap door leading to… what? A cellar or basement, perhaps? I waive Dingus over. The door is right inside the meeting room, which is right next to the entry hall and the attendant's desk. I put my finger to my lips and point down to the door.

Dingus stands guard at the doorway, allowing me to test it. I pull on the ring and the door lifts up. There's a ladder going down into the darkness below the floor. It's perfect! I lower the door back in place only a few seconds before the attendant comes to warn us the building will close in five minutes.

We thank the man, who then turns around and crosses the entryway to the gymnasium side. We have no time to waste.

Dingus flaps his arms to signal the coast is clear and stands guard at the doorway. I open the trap door and follow Nefertiti down the few ladder steps into what turns out to be a short, dark crawl space. It isn't high enough to stand, so we sit cross legged on the dirt floor. Dingus comes down after us. We listen in darkness to the sounds from the floor above. When all is quiet for a sufficiently long time, we venture out of our hiding place.

"Now what?" Dingus says.

"I think we should stay quiet, in case the kid uses this same place. It's old. He might stick with the buildings that he recognizes."

"He wouldn't recognize this one," Nefertiti says. "I saw on the display that it was built in the eighteen hundreds."

I grunt. "Let's just get some sleep." I choose a pew and stretch out on it.

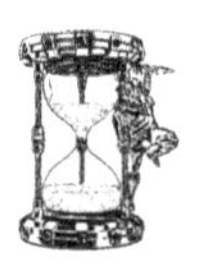

I hear a soft rhythmic breathing from the pew next to me and I know Dingus is in sleep mode. Nefertiti is quiet, but I don't think she's asleep. I attempt to mentally tally our accomplishments thus far, but there doesn't seem to be any. Counting blunders, on the other hand, is not a problem.

We have blown through two of our ten days already. The native is under guard. Our message remains undelivered. Benny is now a prisoner too. We crashed our means of transportation. And we wasted a whole day searching for the boy and found nothing.

"You awake, Nikola?"

I roll toward Nefertiti's voice in the pew behind me. "Yeah."

"I think the veeb's asleep."

"Yes, Dingus is in sleep mode. Don't call him veeb. He doesn't like that."

Nefertiti is quiet for a minute. "I don't mean anything by it. My own mother's a virtual being."

It takes a minute for that to sink in. I sit up. "What? Your mother…"

"I don't mean my dad did something illegal like marry a product of Viarbox. I mean, my real mom works in Tokyo. She's there nine months out of the year, so she got one of those virtual doubles to stand in for her at home."

I don't know what to say to that. "Oh, well. That's cool, I guess."

"Cool? It's not cool! Who wants a veeb making you breakfast or helping you with homework or… or… tucking you in at night?"

"Is that why you don't like Dingus? Because he's not a real person?"

"I just… I just… I don't know. Forget it."

I hear Nefertiti sigh and roll over on the crunchy pew. I don't know how to respond. Or if I should respond. I actually like having a virtual brother. Why not a virtual mom? Dingus could invent a million new ways to outsmart a virtual mom. I think about all the fun we have together. And all the trouble we get into together – usually Dingus' fault.

But, sometimes Dingus gets me into the wrong kind of trouble. Like the tournament. And Daemon. I think about what will happen when we return to the same moment we left. Daemon will still be there. And he'll make a steaming mass of seventh grade pulp out of me – painfully! If only I didn't have to go back to 2076.

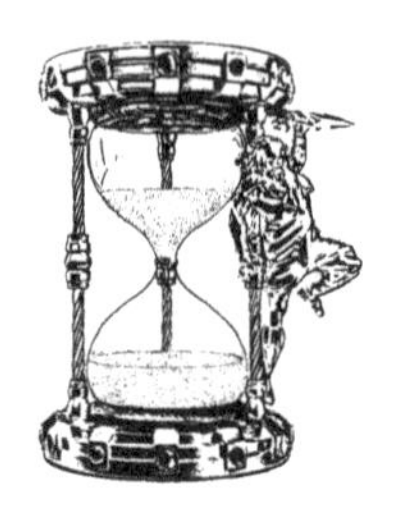

Right between the eyes!

It's the next morning and we are outside. "It's Tuesday," I announce. "We can cover more ground if we split up." I squint at the rising sun. "If I go alone, will you and Dingus be able to keep from fighting without me?"

"No." they both say in unison.

I ignore them. "We can only split into two. We have my pocket pilot and Nefertiti's conferencer to stay in touch."

"Maybe we should sit in one place and watch the people walk past," Dingus says.

"You would think of that." Nefertiti gives Dingus a disgusted look.

"It's not a bad idea," I admit. "When I was little, my mom used to say if I ever got lost I should sit down where I was and she would find me. She said if I wander around one way and she wanders around another, we might never cross paths."

Dingus sticks his tongue out at Nefertiti.

"And what if he's also sitting in one place?" Nefertiti retorts.

"Would you sit in one place if you had a whole new world to explore?"

Dingus sticks his tongue out again.

I sling the pack over my shoulder. "I'll check the park behind Independence Hall for squirrel traps and you guys go…" I waive my hand at nothing in particular, "… somewhere else." I leave before either of them can argue.

I scrutinize every person I see on my way to the park. Once there, I inspect every tree, bush, bench, nook, and cranny for squirrel traps but find nothing. "Nothing," I say to Nefertiti's hologram head that rises out of my pocket pilot.

Nothing here either. Nefertiti reports back. *It's sort of a concrete park. Not a place for rodents to hang out.*

"It was worth a try." I click Nefertiti off and get comfortable on a bench. I scan the park for people, ignoring men and women, but watching for boys. Of the few that go by, I study their expressions, clothes, shoes, the way they walk, their poise and, if I can get close enough to hear, their voices. I hope for anything that might look or sound like an eighteenth-century kid trying to make his way in the twentieth century. I wish I had paid better attention to what the kid looked like in the bronze bowl.

After some time I stand up, stretch, and get the yo-yo out of the backpack. Leaning against a tree, I throw the yo-yo and let it smack back into my hand. I do it again and again. Eventually, I get bored of that and drop my tired arm.

A boy approaches the park and I perk up. He makes brief eye contact with me, stops at the water fountain and drinks. Then he continues to the other side of the park, taking a seat on a bench. He keeps his back to me.

I move to a better spot where I can watch the boy without being seen. Still clutching the yo-yo, and with the pack securely on my shoulder, I grab and click my pocket pilot with my free hand

"Nefertiti," I whisper to her hologram.

Why are you whispering? she answers back.

"I see a boy. He just walked into the park and sat down."

Do you think it's him?

"I don't know yet, but he's alone. That's kind of odd, don't you think? No parents. For this time, I mean. He's pretty young. And he doesn't move like everyone else. Other people move with purpose. He just seemed to be wandering."

Do you want us to come?

"No. Not yet. Let me watch and see what he does."

Okay. Keep us informed.

"I will." I click my pilot and hook it back onto my shorts. I toss the yo-yo to look natural, but keep a steady watch on the boy. His clothes and shoes seem normal for this time, but they don't fit right. The boy's hair is long and ponytailed. Long doesn't seem unusual for this time, but the ponytail does.

The boy bends to pick something up, looks at it, and tosses it back on the ground. He sits another minute. Soon, he stands up and leaves the park with his head down as if looking for something.

I take a few steps to follow when the strong odor of garlic assaults me. The hairs on the back of my neck stand at attention. I turn my head slowly and peer over my shoulder.

Agent Pheloni's fingers twitch on the ends of his raised arms as if ready to grab me. Thinking fast, I turn and throw the yo-yo, hitting him square on the nose. I hear a sickening crack and blood spurts out of his nose. The man falls back while the yo-yo snaps back into my hand. I grab the backpack and hurdle a bench as I dash out of the park.

The Agent is on my heels in a flash.

I zig and zag my way past crowds of people like a transport in the wrong lane. I race across the street against the light. A transport screeches to a halt, nearly hitting me. I pause and see Pheloni cross the same street. The agent hesitates when the transports begin moving again.

I sprint away, looking for places to hide. In the middle of the block, I dive into a revolving door. The interior of the building is immense, like the inside of a shopping mall. Food stands and souvenir shops line the outer walls, with hundreds of café tables in the center. I duck into one of the shops to catch my breath.

I crouch behind a display rack of Liberty Bell mugs and take out my pocket pilot to call Nefertiti.

What's wrong? Was it him? Nefertiti asks.

"I don't know. That agent guy from Chicago showed up. He chased me but I gave him the slip."

Nefertiti's hologram gaze looks beyond my shoulder. I turn to follow it. A woman stands above me with her hands on her hips and a stunned expression on her face.

"Where are you and Dingus?" I ask Nefertiti.

"We're in a concrete park near the river."

"Stay there. I'm coming." I click the pilot and hook it onto my shorts.

"Uh, gotta go," I say to the woman, and slip past her out of the store. I scan the concourse and see Agent Pheloni near the entrance, searching. His eyes meet mine. I take off in the opposite direction happy to see an exit at the far end of the giant room. I dodge the crowd all the way and dive through the back door that someone just opened. Finally I jump down two steps at a time to the sidewalk. I'm now one block away from where I originally entered.

I dash across the street, turn left and run. I curse when I spot Agent Pheloni running up the opposite side of the same street parallel to me. A large truck obscures me when it drives by, so I quickly pull a one-eighty and run alongside the truck back the way it came. I glance back and see Pheloni stop and search.

I turn a corner and run as fast as my legs will go toward the river. This time I don't stop. I run all the way to the park by the waterfront where Dingus and Nefertiti sit and I collapse on the bench, breathless. My clothes stick to my skin and sweat pours off my face.

"What are you doing? What happened?" Nefertiti asks.

"Give him a minute," Dingus says. "Are you okay?"

"Yeah." I pant. "Give me a minute." When I catch my breath I motion for the others to follow me. We crouch behind a statue, hidden from other points in the park.

"Do you think the boy was the one we're looking for?" Dingus asks.

"I don't know."

"Did you talk to him?" Nefertiti asks.

"No. I was watching to see what he did and I started to follow him out of the park. That's when the agent spotted me." I realize I'm still holding the yo-yo. "But I popped him right between the eyes!"

"All right!" Dingus gives me a high-five.

"Yeah, well, he could double back and talk to the lady in the souvenir shop if he didn't already. She heard Nefertiti say you're at the park near the water."

"Where did the boy go?" Dingus asks.

"He went in the other direction. We can't find him now."

"Next time, don't waste time observing," Nefertiti says. "Just walk up to the kid and ask him if he is from another time. If he is, you'll know by his expression even if he doesn't answer."

She's right. I cannot allow anymore slip ups.

Just then, an arm slithers around the statue and grabs Dingus by the neck of his shirt. A second later, Agent Pheloni has both of Dingus' arms behind his back and in cuffs. The agent is panting. Sweat drips from his forehead as he holds Dingus by one arm. He waives a gun at me. "On the ground. Face down. Hands over your heads. Now!"

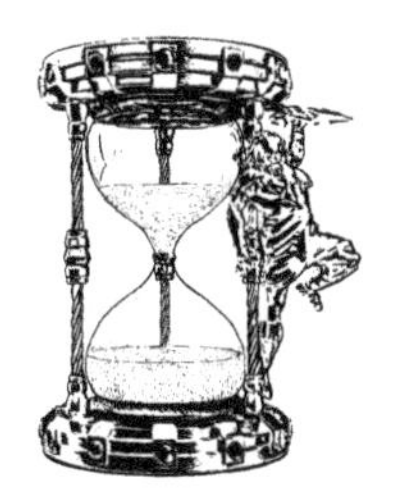

Counting blunders

I do not do as the agent commands. "What do you want with us?"

"You're possible accessories to a crime and you're asking me what *I* want?"

"I don't know what you're talking about." I lean over to Nefertiti and whisper, "Run about two blocks that way and wait for me."

"Don't try anything foolish." He waggles the gun. A trickle of blood leaks from Pheloni's nose and he swipes his sleeve across it. "You'll only make things worse."

I nudge Nefertiti and she bolts.

"I'm an FBI agent!" he shouts. The statue would block any shot he might take. Would he shoot a kid in a public park? I haven't committed a crime. At least I don't think I did.

"This time travel story that Mr. Bennington gave me isn't going to score you points. Not unless you can show me your time machine."

"It's not here," Dingus says.

"Shut up, Ding!"

"What? I didn't say anything."

I roll my eyes. "Fine," I say to Pheloni. "You can keep bigmouth." I turn and bolt in the same direction as Nefertiti, feeling relatively safe on the other side of the big statue. Dingus will make sure he misses his mark if he gets careless with the gun, but I don't hear a shot in any case. Two blocks later, I catch up with Nefertiti.

"Where's Dingus?"

I look around for the best direction to go. "The agent can't run and hold onto Dingus at the same time. Don't worry. I just gave us a head start."

I grab my pocket pilot and click it. When I click it the second time, Dingus is right beside me.

Nefertiti laughs when she catches on to my trick.

"Let's get out of here while he's confused."

We race through the streets, away from the river and into a throng of people. By now, the air is thick and hot. I check my watch. *Two thirty*. It's much later than I expect. I must have been in the other park a long time. Seeing the boy makes me think we're finally making progress. If he's the right kid.

He has to be. I refuse to think otherwise.

"Let's get on one of those public transports that circle the city. We can watch out the windows without being spotted." I lift an eyebrow at Dingus. "We'll grab some soft pretzels for the ride."

Dingus makes no comment. He gets to his feet, ready to go.

I double-check my watch. It's well past lunchtime. At the mere mention of food, Dingus should have reacted like I presented *Rex* with a kid on a plate.

"Are you mad at me?" I ask Dingus. "You know, for leaving you with the agent?"

"Pfff." Dingus waives his hand in dismissal.

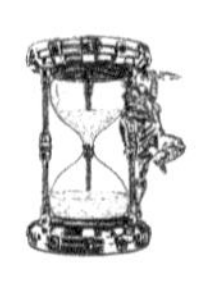

Nefertiti snags a window seat on the left and I find one on the right, across from her. Dingus has to stand, balancing himself with a hand on a pole. A woman glares at him and he glares back until she turns away.

"Ahh," I moan and sink into my seat. I didn't realize how hot I was until I feel the air moving in the open window. On the other hand, I think about how slow the train and then the plane were. This bus ride is ridiculous. I remind myself to watch people out the window. I especially look for the boy I saw in the park. The slow-moving bus is an advantage.

"He ratted us out!" Dingus blurts, standing next to me.

"Who?" I say.

"Benny. You heard the agent. He must have spilled his guts about who we are and why we're here."

"But, it doesn't sound like the agent believed him," Nefertiti offers. "He just thinks we're accomplices to something."

Dingus narrows his eyes to her. "Maybe the agent tortured Benny. You know – used thumb screws or the iron maiden or something."

"Dingus!" Nefertiti flinches.

"Maybe he's all bloody and mangled. Maybe he's being tortured right now."

"Cut it out, Ding," I say. I lean past him to talk to Nefertiti. "He's not being tortured."

"How do you know?" he says.

"Because this isn't the Middle Ages, Technoid. Benny will be fine."

Dingus says nothing, but narrows his eyes at Nefertiti.

When the transport is deep in the city, far outside of the old part, I feel like we made a mistake. I'm sure the boy will stick to his familiar surroundings and I assumed the transport would too. But I keep my eyes peeled. Nefertiti and Dingus stop bickering and keep watch as well. We watch for Pheloni, too. If we know where the agent is, it will make finding the kid a little easier.

The transport completes its loop and drives back down Market Street, past Seventh and toward Sixth. I perk up. "Pay attention, guys," I whisper. "I think we're back in the old city."

By now, we pretty well know our way around the area. When we ride past the park, I scour the area for the boy, but he is long gone. There's no sign of the agent either. The bus completes the historic loop and starts heading back into the bigger part of the city.

I sigh. "Maybe this isn't such a good idea. Sitting still in one place was working much better. I think we should get off now before the transport gets further outside this section of the city. It takes so long to go all the way around and it's not that late. We're just wasting time."

"Maybe you're right," Nefertiti says.

"He's right," Dingus confirms.

We hop off the bus and backtrack the couple blocks on foot. The sky has grown dark.

"Looks like it's going to rain." Just as Nefertiti says that I feel the first heavy raindrop slap my forehead.

"Whose idea was it to get off the transport?" Dingus says. The few drops quickly turn into a downpour.

I look up at the falling rain. The cold water rinses away the sweat of the day. If feels good on my face and I don't care that my clothes are soaked through in seconds.

We walk a few blocks until we realize we're the only ones in the rain. So we move to a raised parking lot where we can watch pedestrians without being conspicuous. For three more hours we stay in that spot, seeing nothing that makes us look twice. We don't find the agent either. Not many people are out walking in the rain, and those who are, use umbrellas. From our vantage point, we can't see faces.

I am happy when the rain stops, but my wet clothes have long since changed from refreshing to sticky to gross.

"Look on the bright side," Nefertiti says. "At least we got our clothes washed again."

"Big deal," Dingus says. "Why are girls so obsessed with being clean?"

"Humans can't click themselves clean," Nefertiti says.

"Or dry," I say as I click my pocket pilot to refresh Dingus. At least one of us can be dry.

Oddly, maybe even thankfully, Dingus makes no remark about being hungry.

Since it was so easy before and we don't have a better plan, we sneak into the same Quaker Meeting House. We find an assortment of coats and sweaters in a closet so Nefertiti and I change our clothes. I wear a coat that fits me like a bathrobe. Nefertiti wears a ladies jacket on top and a knitted cardigan sweater around her waist. She says we shouldn't lay our wet clothes on the antique pews so we hang them in the sanitation room instead.

We each grab a pew and lay down to sleep.

"What if we never find him?" I say, looking up at the wooden beams over my head. "I mean, is there a point when we should just give up and go on to California?"

"I wonder how the native is doing," Dingus says.

"I wonder how Benny is doing," Nefertiti says.

"That traitor?" Dingus sits up in his pew. "Why should we care? He ratted us out."

"He didn't mean it. He was trying to help," Nefertiti yells back. "And don't forget, we're using his money."

"No we're not." Dingus lays back down in the pew. "If we were, we wouldn't be hiding out in this church."

"We have to save the money for important things," I say.

"Yeah." Nefertiti pokes her head up at Dingus. "Like feeding *your* appetite."

"*My* food doesn't cost you anything." He sticks his tongue out at her.

"Let's change the subject." I don't want to deal with their bickering. "How are we even going to get to California? We don't have Benny's transport anymore."

"I don't know. Should we dump out the backpack again?" she asks.

"No. There's nothing in it."

Nefertiti sits up. "Maybe we should pick a deadline to finish here so we still have time to do what we need to do in California. We can figure out how to get there later. How much more time do we need here?"

"A million years," I say. "We didn't get anywhere yet. I wish I would have seen that kid again. I had a good feeling about him."

"What was he wearing?" Nefertiti asks.

"I don't know. Regular clothes, I guess."

"Regular for his time or this time?" Dingus sits up.

"This time. He was about our age – maybe a little younger."

"What made you think it was the right kid?" Dingus asks.

"The way he looked at things. Like it was new and different. The way he walked. His clothes could have been swiped out of a lost-and-found box." I lift my shoulder and drop it again. "I don't know. I just had a feeling."

"Did you hear him talk? Did he have an accent?" Nefertiti asks.

"He didn't talk."

"I wonder what he's doing now," Nefertiti says. "I wonder where he's sleeping – how he's getting along. Is he afraid?"

"Maybe he's hurt – or dead!" Dingus says.

"Don't say that!" Nefertiti reaches across the pew to smack Dingus in the arm but she misses.

"Hey, it's true!" Dingus defends himself, "If you were from the year seventeen seventy-six and suddenly found yourself two hundred years in the future, you wouldn't know what can hurt you and what can't, right?"

"No." When Nefertiti speaks, I hear a bump over our heads in the wooden balcony. We all sit up and look toward the sound. No one makes a peep. Then I see something move in the balcony. It's dark and difficult to see, but I get a sinking feeling.

"It's him! It's the agent. Run!"

All three of us jump out of our pews and race toward the doorway, tripping over our oversized clothing along the way.

A small voice echoes off the wooden walls. "Wait. Doona go away." I skid to a stop on the floor boards. Dingus and Nefertiti stop beside me.

Nefertiti takes a step back into the room. "Who are you?"

I whisper, "It's him."

A small figure leans over the wooden rail above us. "I dinna mean to spy. But, methinks ye ken what has happened to me."

I step forward.

"Go ahead," Nefertiti says. "Ask."

"Are you..." I think about the best way to phrase the question. "Did you get here... by magic?"

The pause stretches on forever.

"Aye." The small voice whispers.

"It is him!" Nefertiti says.

"Yes!" I want to spike something in victory, but don't want to scare the kid. "Yes, and we can help you. It's our fault you're here. We've been looking for you. We're from the year twenty seventy-six."

The boy peers over the rail. "How can that be?"

I swallow the lump in my throat. "It's a long story. Come down and we'll tell you all about it."

The boy comes down the creaky stairs. I study him at close range. His face. His hair. His eyes. He's nothing special, just a small boy. But I feel like an archaeologist uncovering a priceless artifact. A small piece of history standing right in front me.

"What's your name?" I ask.

"I am Jamie." He points to my clothes. "Is that how people dress in yer time?" His thick brogue and the cool way he rolled his r's tells me he isn't British.

Nefertiti looks down at her ensemble and answers his question. "We got caught in the rain and washed our clothes."

Jamie nods as if he's done the same thing.

"I'm Nikola. This is Dingus. And this is Nefertiti. Were you here last night?"

"No. I went to Christ's Church the first night. In the winter past, a man let me sleep there. So I tried again. But that was afore…" He holds his arms out, presenting his new situation. He lets them drop in defeat. "A woman chased me away. I slept in the alley instead. But, the ground is verra hard and cold. I would have gone to the woods and made a leaf mold… but, I couldna find the woods. So I tried this place today. I stole up to yon loft afore ye came in."

"Excellent choice!" Dingus says.

"It took a couple days, but our think-like-a-homeless-person logic paid off." Nefertiti beams with self-pride at her wisdom.

"Yeah. You don't know how good it is that we found you." Relief pours over me. "I didn't think I'd get a second chance. I saw you at the park earlier."

Jamie nods. "Aye. A man chased ye away. Was he the landowner, then?"

"No, but I guess we have a lot to tell you."

Everyone settles into the pews and I explain everything that happened — the hourglass that's really a time travel program, the displacements, the native and the priest, Daemon sending us to the same time, and our trek from Chicago to find him – right up to this very moment. "We came here to help you get back to your own time."

Back?" Jamie's eyebrows draw together.

"Yeah. We came here to send you home. Y'know. Seventeen seventy-six."

The boy stands up and glares at me. I try to read his face. Is it fear? Anger?

"What's wrong?" I say.

Jamie doesn't answer.

He bolts. He runs out of the meeting room, into the lobby and I hear the main doors of the Meeting House crash open.

"That didn't go very well."

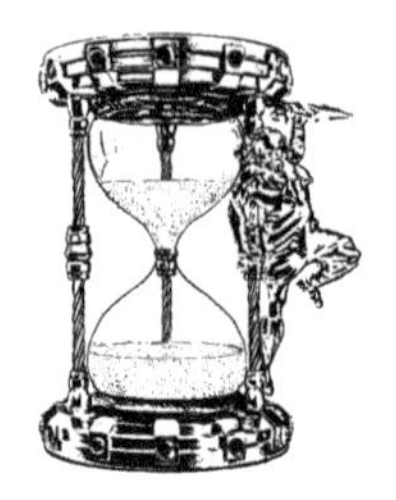

More game tools in a marble bag

I sail out of the room in Jamie's wake. As I burst through the front doors into the night air, I spot him running along the inside of the high red brick wall. There is enough light from the street and nearby buildings to see. The gates are closed and Jamie is too small to climb them. He follows the perimeter of the yard and I run after him.

Nefertiti's long legs catch her up quickly and she overtakes me, gaining on Jamie. By the time I round the corner of the yard, Nefertiti already has him in the grass, fighting to hold him down. Jamie kicks and punches, and I dive into the fray.

"Stop!" I say, avoiding a kick. "Stop! What's wrong? Why did you run?"

"I willna go back!" he shouts as he struggles. "I willna go back!" He continues to fight and Nefertiti and I continue to hold him down until the fight finally drains out of him. "I willna go back," he repeats, weakly.

"Shh." Nefertiti soothes the boy even though she continues to sit on top of him. "It's okay. Maybe we don't have to send you back." She speaks gently. "Let's talk about it first, okay?"

"Gerroff me," Jamie says.

"You won't run?"

"No."

"Promise?"

"Aye."

"Get off him." I say, watching Jamie's eyes as I speak to Nefertiti. "He won't run."

Nefertiti gets off the boy and sits in the grass beside him. Dingus finally catches up to us, panting. He joins the rest of us on the grass.

"Why don't you want to go home?" I ask.

Jamie lifts his face to the dark sky. His gaze follows the lights of what must be a transport that is low to the ground. When it is gone he turns back to me. "Tis better here."

"Won't you miss your family?" I ask.

He lifts a shoulder. "I have nae kin."

"Where do you live? Who takes care of you?"

"I am me own keeper. I live here… Except… no right here." Jamie shakes his head at his botched explanation. "Da died and Mama and me come to America. Then she died and…" he shrugs, "I havena anywhere to go."

I'm horrified. I can't imagine losing one parent let alone both. "I'm sorry," I say sincerely. I never lost anyone and have no idea what else to say. Anything more seems… impossible. I rest my hand on his back. "Can you get foster parents or something?"

He looks at me like he's not sure what I said. Finally he responds. "People sent me to a place for boys with no parents. They gave me a pallet to sleep on and food to eat. But they beat me every day – even when I dinna do anything! So I ran away.

"On the streets, I steal food when I have to. If they cotch me, they will cut off my hand or brand my face to let people know I am a thief. Some thieves get hangit." He touches his neck and Nefertiti gasps.

"But, here..." he pauses and holds out his arms. "I watch people steal. No one pays them any mind. They still have their hands. Their faces havena brand mark. The noose doesna find their necks." He lifts one shoulder. "I willna go hungry here."

"How long have you been on your own?" Nefertiti asks.

He looks to the sky as if thinking. "This is my third summer."

Nefertiti gasps. "Three years on your own? Well, you won't be alone ever again, I promise!" She pulls the boy into her arms and squeezes. He squirms to get loose, but she holds on.

"Can we bring him home with us?" Dingus asks me.

I don't know what to say. Jamie isn't a stray dog or cat. I can't click the boy off and on like Dingus. "I don't know."

"It wouldn't be right to send him back," Nefertiti says, looking at me over Jamie's squirming shoulder. "And it wouldn't be right to leave him here either. He's just as homeless here as he was in his own time."

"Let him go, Nefertiti," I say, taking pity on the boy. She does. "What about our time? Won't he have the same problem there?"

"*We* can look after him," she says.

"My parents would kill me."

"Mine won't." Nefertiti turns to the boy. "Do you want to come forward to our time, Jamie?"

"Aye! I am strong. I can clean yer stables, watch yer kettle, fetch and carry wood. I can cotch fish and squirrels and rabbits."

"No, Jamie," she says. "You won't have to do any of those things. But we might have to keep you hidden. We'll work out the details later. Are you sure you want to do this?"

"Aye."

"Then it's settled. Now let's go back and get some sleep."

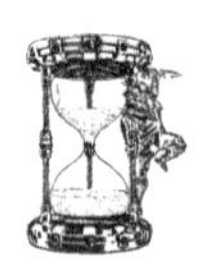

Early Wednesday morning, four of us sneak out of the Quaker Meeting House. The previous day's rain brings a clear crispness to the air. Except for a few puddles, the ground is already dry in the July heat.

We buy breakfast sandwiches and orange juice and then find an alley that seems a likely place to eat and talk in private. I lean against a concrete wall and enjoy the coolness of the shade. After eating our breakfast, we all stuff our trash in the bag and turn our attention to more important matters.

I dump the backpack on the cement in front of us. Jamie immediately reaches into the pile but I stop him. "In our time," I explain, "we play Viarbox games. That's the earpiece and here are some games." I hold up a few cartridges. "They're a lot of fun, but you have to do stuff that's sometimes scary."

"Like fight aliens or dinosaurs," Dingus says.

"A-liens? Dinnasars?"

"Great big monsters."

Jamie's eyes spring wide open.

"It's not real. It's just a game." I put down the cartridges and pick up the earpiece. "If you get scared, you just press this button and they go away."

Jamie reaches for the cartridge with a picture of airplanes on it. "May I try this one?"

"Maybe later." I put a hand out to stop him from further investigation. "Right now we have to think. Sometimes when we play Viarbox games, there's a certain task we have to do in a certain amount of time. It's a lot like what the three of us are doing right now. We started with ten days and our task is to find three people…"

"That's you and two others." Nefertiti says. "We already found you."

I continue. "Now we have to move on to the next level. We have to go to California so we can help the next person. In a Viarbox game, you get certain tools to help you. This stuff right here is all we brought with us, so these are our tools. It's kind of dumb stuff but it got us here so far."

"Don't forget, Benny gets to keep them – if he's not hanging in a torture chamber by his toes."

Jamie gasps. "What has he done?"

"Nothing. Cut it out, Dingus. As I was saying," I continue, "the only help we get is from our brains and our tools and anything else we find along the way. These are the tools we have now. We have to figure out how to get to California. That's three thousand miles away."

Jamie's eyes fly open. "Three thousand... that's... how far is that?"

"It might as well be on the other side of the moon," I say. "That's why we have to think real hard. We came here in a transport... er... airplane, but we crashed it."

"Airplane?"

"It's one of those things you see flying around in the sky." I point to one approaching in the distance. There must be an airport nearby because the planes are big and low in the sky like they were in Chicago.

Jamie watches the plane approach and get lower until it drops out of sight behind a building. Then he turns to me. "I have some tools. Would you like to see?"

"Sure." I say. "It can't be worse than the stuff I brought."

Jamie pulls a brown leather pouch out of his shirt. He unties the cord around it and dumps the contents on the ground next to the larger pile. A few coins jingle as they hit the cement. Several small wooden balls clatter and threaten to roll away until Jamie nudges them back to the pile. There's a piece of cork with two fish hooks stuck into it and some string wound around it. Another cork and two rocks bounce onto the ground. And there are two tiny, beautifully carved wooden birds.

Nefertiti scoops up the birds. "They're beautiful!"

"They were Mama's."

Nefertiti inspects them at close range. She hands them gently to Jamie, who stuffs them into the leather pouch with a bit less care.

I pick up one of the wooden balls. "What are these?"

"Those are marbles. Tis a game." Jamie takes one of the marbles from my hand and flicks it on the ground hard enough to knock a small pebble. "If that was yer marble, ye would be out of the circle. Try it."

I politely give it a try. I flick and the marble flops to the ground.

"Try it again." Jamie demonstrates how to hold the marble in the crook of his finger and flick it with his thumb.

I flick it a little better this time. The marble taps the rock.

Dingus picks up one of the other marbles and gives it a try. The marble rolls across the alley and he has to get up and chase after it.

I put my marble back on the pile to check out the coins. I'm pretty sure paper money is worth more than coins. And our paper money is dwindling fast. The coins likely won't last long. I pick up several and inspect them. Ten cents, five cents... I check the dates on two of them: 1972 and 1969. Jamie must have found them here.

Jamie drops the toy transport he was holding and takes a copper coin from me. He looks at it and says, "This is only worth one," and hands it back. "I tried to buy food with it, but 'twas no enough. All of them together were no enough." He lifts a shoulder. "It willna help get us to Cali...feeni..."

Dingus holds his hand out. I assume he wants the coins, so I drop them into his palm. He picks through them and then whistles softly through his teeth. He holds one up.

"What's up, Ding?" I ask.

"This one." Dingus holds one of the coins up to Jamie. "Did you find it here or did you bring it with you?"

"It was my mam's."

"I thought so." Dingus flipped the coin in his hand. "It's different from the others. Bigger. And it looks like it was minted differently. The lines aren't as clean and detailed as the others. And the date is 1765. Did you have this with you when…"

"Yes," he says.

"Then it's an antique in this time!" I say.

Dingus nods.

I take the coin and inspect it. Dingus is right. It is different. I don't understand the writing on it. One side has a picture of a man… no, a lady. Well, it's either a man or really ugly lady. I flip it over to see a two-headed bird squashed under a shield. And the date is clear. 1765.

Dingus takes the coin back. He holds it up close to his eye and blinks. Then he closes his eyes for a few seconds and reopens them. "I found a match. It's called a Maria Theresa thaler." He holds the coin up to the side showing the – yes, it is a very ugly woman. "She was a queen or emperor or something," Dingus continues. "The point is, it's old."

"That means it's a collectible," I explain to Jamie, who looks puzzled. "It might be worth more than its normal value."

"You can't sell Jamie's money!" Nefertiti protests. "He might have been saving it for something."

True. He held onto it for three whole years without spending it.

"If it is useful to ye, then use it," Jamie says. "I tried to buy food with it one time. The woman accused me of thievery. I got away, but kenned it would be of no use to me." He throws a pebble across the alley and it clicks against the brick wall of the building.

"If it's worth a lot, we could buy our own transport and drive to California," Dingus says.

"Oh no." Nefertiti says. "I've been in an airplane with you. There's no way I'm getting in a rolling transport with you."

"Rolling transport." Jamie says. "Is that what ye call yon carriages with no horse to pull them?"

"Yeah," Nefertiti says. "And don't get in one if Dingus is behind the wheel."

"It wasn't my fault we crashed!" Dingus shouts.

"You can't go faster than the guy in front of you," I say. "And they don't have altitude meters. They just roll around."

"Ye went in a rolling transport?" Jamie asks.

"Just in a Viarbox game," I say.

"So how can we buy a ri-ri-ride to Chicago?" Dingus asks. "They have ro-ro-rolling transports, airplanes, trains, subways and taxis in this time. Can we re-re-rent one?"

I narrow my eyes at Dingus. Dingus tips his head, thumps his chest with his fist, and burps.

"Better?" I ask.

"Yeah. Much."

I take out my pocket pilot and point it at Dingus. "I'm just going to refresh you, okay?"

Dingus nods.

I tip my chin in Jamie's direction, and Nefertiti distracts him with a question about marbles.

I click Dingus off, wait a few seconds, and then click him back on.

"Say something."

Dingus shrugs. "Say what?"

"I don't know. Just talk so I know you're okay.

Dingus recites the Viarbox virtual friend's product disclaimer.

I have no idea what all the legal mumbo jumbo means, but Dingus doesn't stammer at all while saying it. That's a relief.

But, it's odd that he chose to recite a disclaimer instead of whining about food.

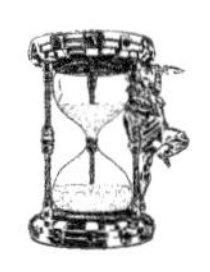

The four of us wander the city to look for an antiques shop. We finally find one with a sign in the window indicating they buy and sell coins.

I hop onto the stoop and open the door. Dingus, Nefertiti and Jamie follow me inside. The dark room is cluttered with retro advertisements, Coca-Cola memorabilia, old jewelry, tin toys, small furniture items and, most importantly, a coin counter.

A man carries a box into the room from the doorway at the back. He stops when he sees us. "Can I help you?"

"We have a coin to sell. Can you take a look?" I hold the coin up for the man to see. He heaves the box onto the floor without looking at the coin. "What year is it from?"

"1765," I say.

"What country?"

"I don't know." I push the coin under the man's nose, ugly lady side up. The man leans in and squints. His eyes grow wide and he stands up with a jerk.

I follow him to the glass counter and place the coin on top. He turns on a light with a magnifier connected to it and flips the coin over and then over again. Bending down, he roots around under the counter and brings up a thick book. He flips through several pages and then several more. Finally he stabs a page with his finger. "There it is!" he says. "Take a look." He turns the book around for me to see.

"Maria Theresa thaler, just like you said, Dingus."

"Of course." Dingus says.

"A Maria Theresa thaler," the man mutters with reverence. "The ones dated 1780 aren't worth as much, but… 1765." He holds the coin on the tip of one finger and runs his thumb lightly over the face of it. "Where did you get this?"

"It's Jamie's," I say.

Dingus steps up with a story. "He found it a couple years ago," he explains. "We waited long enough for the owner to claim it. I mean, you can't exactly advertise or you'll have all kinds of weirdoes calling, right? He waited two years. It's his now."

"Do your parents know?" the man asks.

"Here we go again," I whisper. "He's a foster kid," I say louder to the man.

"The kind of money you'd make on a sale like that is too much for a child to handle," the man informs us. "I need to deal with an adult."

"How about a trade?" I suggest.

The man shifts his gaze to Jamie and back to me. "What kind of trade?" He opens his arms, displaying everything in his store. "Have a look around."

"Not that kind of trade," I say. "We need a ride to California."

"Are you joking?"

"No joke," I say. "We need to get to California as fast as possible."

"You're kids."

I sigh. "We're aware of that."

"Don't they allow kids in California?" Dingus asks.

"Please don't think of us as kids," Nefertiti pleads.

"Are you in some kind of trouble?"

"We will be if we don't get to California," I say.

"If this is real, it might be worth a ride to California," the man says.

"If you're willing to take a chance on us, we're willing to part with it for the price of a ride."

"I don't understand," the man says. "It's not stolen, is it?"

"This? Of course not," Dingus chimes in. "It's Jamie's. He found it a long time ago."

"If we stole it," Nefertiti offers, "Don't you think we'd be asking for more than a ride somewhere? If mean, wouldn't a criminal be greedier than that?"

The man rocks his head from side to side as if weighing that wisdom.

"We just need someone who will trust us enough to help," I say.

"Call your dad for me right now," the man says to Jamie.

Jamie looks to Dingus for help.

"He can't," Dingus says.

"Why not?"

"He doesn't have a dad," Dingus says.

"You don't understand and we don't have time to explain," I plead. "We need a ride to California. As soon as possible. If you can't do this, then we're back to square one and we'll never make it home."

"Home?" the man asks. "You don't live here? Were you left behind? Abandoned? I can call child services. They'll take care of you… get you where you need to go."

"Please," I say. "Please don't ask questions. It gets complicated. We just want to go home. That's all. And if you'll take us, then you can keep the coin."

"Please," Nefertiti says.

"Please," Jamie adds.

The man flips the coin in the palm of his hand. He sets it back on the counter slowly. "It's in incredible condition. I'd like to know where you found it. Where was it stored all these years?"

"It doesn't matter," I say.

"What happens in California that you have to make it on time?"

"No! No questions," I say. "This is a blind faith thing. You just have to trust us."

"It's a pretty big carrot you're holding there." The man stares at us, lined up in front of him. He looks into each of our eyes as if sizing up our truthfulness. His sigh is so deep it lifts both shoulders nearly to his ears. Finally, he lets his shoulders drop and gives his answer.

"No. I could be charged with kidnapping." The man sets the coin on the counter. "I can find a buyer and get you the money. That's the best I can offer."

"How long will that take?" I ask.

"A few weeks."

"Never mind." I lift the coin off the counter, hand it to Jamie, and head for the door.

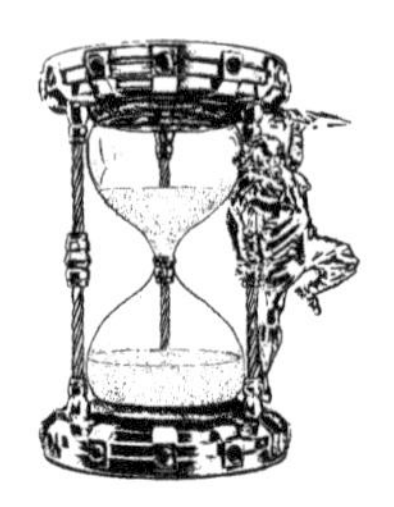

Drrriving in a rrrolling trrransport, aye

Angry and frustrated, I'm even more determined. I lead everyone through one more look-at-the-dumb-stuff-in-the-backpack session.

The assortment has grown to include the maps and brochures from the hotel. One has regional train routes, which gives me the idea of taking a transcontinental train, but it's not exactly nonstop and the trip could take days. Just buying a ticket without an adult will probably call attention to us and someone will associate us with the airplane story in the paper.

But the regional line, which we can get on for a token, will put us in walking distance to the Pennsylvania turnpike, which runs east to west. Hopefully, we'll find a better option on foot. If we have to hitchhike all the way to California, then so be it.

Nefertiti balks at my terrible and dangerous idea, but she trots along to the train station when I refuse to stop. If she has a better idea, she doesn't voice it and I am not in a waiting mood.

About an hour later, the four of us hop off the train and begin the long trek west along Pennsylvania Route 76.

We stick to the woods that runs along the edge to avoid attracting unwanted attention. That makes it slow going. I can't believe I had been upset about the slow airplane, trains and bus. We're traveling at a snail's pace now. It's too depressing to think about. So I worry about Dingus instead.

It is well after lunch and my own belly is rumbling, but Dingus hasn't said a word.

"Dingus." I fall into step alongside him. "Are you okay?"

"I'm fine."

"Maybe…" I hesitate. "Maybe I should turn you off for a day or two. Maybe you're just overdoing it."

"No!" Dingus says. "I'm fine."

"Okay, I won't turn you off unless you ask. But, Dingus, talk to me, okay? Tell me what you're feeling. Tell me what's wrong."

Dingus rubs his belly. "My stomach feels weird."

"What do you think's going on?"

Dingus shakes his head. "I don't know."

"Do you think he's got the flu or some kind of bug?" Nefertiti asks.

"Dingus can't catch human diseases. If he vomits, it's because he wants to."

Nefertiti rolls her eyes. "Veebs."

Actually, it's the first time I ever saw Dingus involuntarily sick. But I promised not to turn him off unless he asks and a promise is a promise.

Night comes and we have to rest or collapse on the spot. Too bad we're exhausted. We probably could move faster walking closer to the road in the dark. Camping without the right gear is not fun. Jamie is the only one who doesn't complain. He piles up a bunch of leaves, makes a cozy nest in the center, curls himself up, and sleeps like he hasn't a care in the world. The rest of us make our own nests in the same fashion. It's not so bad. It's softer than the pews and smells of pine and other earthy scents. I am so exhausted from walking all day, neither the ticking clock nor worry over Dingus keeps me awake.

I feel like I had just laid down when it is suddenly Thursday morning. I hurt all over. And by the sound of her groans, so does Nefertiti. I sit up and rub my eyes, which immediately focus on Jamie. He's standing a few feet away, mouth hanging open with a finger pointing to Dingus' left leg. Or the spot where Dingus' left leg should be if he still had one.

Dingus looks momentarily shocked himself when he looks down and sees what Jamie is pointing at. I jump out of my nest and reach out to help Dingus stand up. As Dingus rises, his leg reappears.

"You okay?" I ask.

"Yeah, I think so." Dingus shakes his leg for reassurance. "Feels okay."

"You hungry?"

"No."

Okay, that does it. Something is clearly wrong, and I don't think even Dingus knows what it might be. Nefertiti and I will have to keep a close watch on him.

Jamie is still staring. "It's okay, Jamie." I turn to Dingus. "I guess we should explain you."

Dingus nods.

I explain virtual beings and Jamie accepts the information with the same enthusiastic interest as the other new wonders he has experienced in the past few days. Dingus is just another to add to the pile.

After a quick breakfast of cold water from a nearby stream, we pick up where we left off last night. Walking. Somewhere in Pennsylvania. Counting down the miles to California.

As worrying as it is, I'm grateful Dingus doesn't whine about food. It helps me to keep my mind off my own stomach. When the sun is high in the sky we come to a rest stop. So we stop to rest.

Jamie lingers in the men's room, fascinated with the toilets and sinks. The rest of us sit at a picnic table facing the parking lot, eating vending machine crackers and drinking canned soft drinks. My heart lifts when I see Dingus make several copies of the crackers, but it sinks again when he merely stuffs them in his pocket.

I get my mind back on more important tasks. I was hoping we might stow away on one of the large hauler transports we see on the highway. But, there aren't any on the parking lot just now. If we wait long enough, one might show up. But how long is too long to wait? I hate sitting and doing nothing.

I see a smaller box-shaped transport backed into a parking space. The back door of the transport is open and two teenage girls sit side-by-side on the edge, dangling their feet.

One girl wears a multi-colored skirt and flowery shirt with long, wide sleeves. A mass of bushy brown hair sticks out from beneath a blue and white bandana tied around her head.

The other girl has straight blond hair beneath a red bandana. Her jeans have more patches than denim and her shirt is nothing more than a red strip of elastic fabric stretched across her chest. I look down and think my animated lucky Indy car shirt would be less noticeable. But Nefertiti insists I wear it inside-out to avoid attracting attention.

I watch the girls talk and laugh with each other. Inside my head, I swear I can hear a clock ticking. We have to get going soon. My legs ache so bad I can't bear the thought of more walking. But we have to keep moving.

Then the two girls hop off the back of their transport. One picks up a red cooler from the parking lot and crams it into the transport before closing the door. That's when I see it.

The crude sign in the back window of the transport says, "California or Bust."

"Wait!" I shout to the girls without conscious thought.

"What are you doing?" Nefertiti says, but I'm already running.

With the drivers' side door open and one foot inside, the girl in the skirt stops and looks up when I call out a second time. She watches me approach.

"Are you going to California?" I say, panting when I reach the transport.

"Uh huh." She nods.

"Can we…" I turn and gesture toward Nefertiti and Dingus, happy to see that Jamie has joined them, "Can we come with you?"

The girl turns to her friend, who is getting into the transport on the other side. The friend pulls her eyebrows together and looks at each of us. "They're rug rats!" Then she lifts a shoulder. "But they look pretty harmless."

The first girl turns back to me. "Do you have any bread?" she asks. "No one rides free."

I shake my head. "No bread, but we have money. We can stop somewhere and buy bread."

"Is he for real?" The second girl says from inside the transport. The girl on the driver's side laughs. "A little square, but he'll do." She turns back to me. "I already gassed up so you can get the next round, okay?"

"Yeah, sure," I say.

"Your friends coming or what?"

I waste no time. "Come on!" I waive to the others. When they hesitate, I call again. "Do you want to walk to California or ride?"

The three jump off the bench and run to the parking lot.

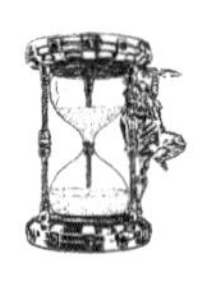

The girls pile two coolers, a guitar case, two cardboard boxes, and assorted clothing into the far back so we all can squeeze in. There are no seat belts. There aren't even seats. Much of the floor is piled high with blankets, pillows and more clothes, making a lumpy nest. The four of us sit cross legged on top of everything.

"Hang on." When the transport lurches into movement, I grab the back of the driver's seat to keep from falling into Nefertiti. The girl who is driving pulls out of the space and we are on our way.

Once on the highway, the driver glances into the rear view mirror at me. "I'm Jenny," she says. She tilts her head toward her friend. "This is Amy."

Amy turns around and smiles.

"Thanks for letting us ride with you," I say politely to Amy.

"How old are you?" she asks.

Uh oh. The old parents routine is about to start. At least we're already in the transport. Hopefully the girls won't kick us out until we get to another rest stop.

"Twelve."

"Thirteen!" Nefertiti shouts over me. I'm relieved that Nefertiti is older. It might be an important one-year difference.

"How about you?" I turn the table on the girls to keep them from probing further.

"I'm seventeen." Jenny tips her head toward the passenger seat. "Amy's sixteen."

Amy turns around. "We're going to be big stars."

"Are you actresses?" Nefertiti says, sounding impressed.

"Singers," Jenny says. The guitar case in the back suddenly makes sense.

"So what's your bag?" Jenny says into the rear view mirror. "What's calling you to California?"

I shrug and look over at Dingus, hoping he can come up with a winner. He just lifts a shoulder. I decide to evade the question with another tactic. "I'm Nikola. This is Nefertiti, Dingus and Jamie." I point to each in turn.

"Nefertiti?" Jenny asks. "I like that. I mean, how boring is Jenny, right? And what's Dingus short for?"

"Nothing. I'm just Dingus."

"Your parents actually named you Dingus?" Jenny giggles, then sobers when she looks in the mirror. "Hey, it's cool, man," she says. "Don't get your panties in a wad."

Dingus' face has turned a deep shade of red.

Amy turns practically all the way around in the seat to look at Jamie behind her. "You're pretty young to be running away from home. What did he say is your name?"

"I am called Jamie. My Christian name is James Column Robert MacRobert Campbell. We are not running away. We're running toward. Weel, actually, we are no running 'tall. Ye are driving us in yer rolling transport."

Amy and Jenny look at each other. Four eyebrows shoot into the air. "Righteous!" they shout in unison. Jenny looks over her shoulder. "Say something else! Say something with r's in it."

"Something with r's in it." Jamie repeats her words. Then, realizing what she wanted, he adds with exaggeration, "Rrrolling trrransport." He is rewarded with giggles from the girls.

"That is the coolest accent I ever heard. Is that Scottish?" Jenny says.

"Aye."

"Far out! What are you doing in America? Why are you going to California? What are you doing with these guys?"

"How long will it take to get there?" I interrupt before Jamie attempts to answer her string of questions.

Jenny sobers. It takes a moment for her to absorb the change of subject. "As long as we want it to. This is an adventure," she says.

"We need to get there fast," I say. "As fast as possible. If someone's life depended on it, how fast could we get there?"

"Are you in some kind of trouble?" Amy turns around in her seat and looks worried, but interested.

"No, not trouble. Just in a hurry."

"Then thumbing it probably isn't your best bet. But, we could drive straight through. Maybe three or four days, stopping to sleep."

"Dingus, Nefertiti and I can share the driving so we don't have to stop to sleep."

"You drive?" Jenny asks, incredulously.

"Jalopy Junction," Jamie says, helpfully.

"Yes," I say. "We can all help. Except Jamie. He's never driven here before."

"What do you mean, 'here'?"

"They drive on the wrong side of the road in Scotland." Dingus says.

"They do?" Jamie looks at Dingus.

"Far out," Amy says.

Jenny looks at me through the mirror. "It would still take two or three days to get there even if we only stop for gas and bathrooms."

I mentally calculate the time. It is noon Thursday. We have to make it back to Chicago by Wednesday of next week. Two days driving might get us to California by Saturday afternoon. We already know where to find the priest, assuming he's still at the white church. We can be back on our way to Chicago the same day. If we have to drive all the way to Chicago, it would take nearly two more days, which can get us there around Tuesday morning. We can use the rest of Tuesday and Wednesday morning to get the native and Benny out of lockup — if they're still there. Then we make it back to our marks by Wednesday afternoon.

That is completely full of holes and doesn't give us a buffer for things to go wrong. But, conceivably, it could work. I shrug at the tight schedule. What other choice do we have? It's still better than walking. I make a mental note to watch for faster options along the way. "Let's do it," I say. "Can we make it by Saturday morning?"

"Are you for real?" Jenny says into the mirror.

"Yeah. We really need to be in San Diego as quickly as possible. You game?"

Jenny looks at Amy.

"Yeah!" Amy smiles. "It'll be like that movie, *It's a Mad, Mad World*, or something like that. I mean, there's no million bucks at the end, but it could be fun." She turns back to look at me. "There's no million bucks at the end is there?"

I shake my head.

"Too bad."

"Count us in." Jenny says.

Amy switches on a portable radio, tunes in and out until she settles on a station and they sing along to the crackly music. *Just call me Angel, of the morning…*

I calculate our speed by watching the mile markers and noting the time. Then I remember the dashboard has a gage. I lean over Jenny's shoulder to see it and the gage confirms my calculations. I sigh and leaned back. I don't want to be rude, but I can't help wondering why the gage goes up to eighty miles per hour and we're only going forty-five. Sure, it's faster than walking but this is ridiculous.

An hour later, the radio turns to static. Amy turns it off.

It's quiet for a few minutes. Then Jenny breaks the silence. "Are your parents a drag? Is that why you're running away?"

I shrug, not sure what *drag* meant. "We told you, we're not running away."

"Yes," Nefertiti answers in a huff. "My mother's a drag."

"Your mother is the best kind there is, Nef. The... er..." I can't say *virtual* in front of Jenny and Amy.

"Hmpf." Nefertiti folds her arms across her chest and sits back.

Jenny glances into the mirror. "My parents are divorced. Every Friday night, Mom goes out on a date like she's some kind of teenager. It's embarrassing." Her eyes look back at the road. "I wonder sometimes if she even remembers she has a daughter."

Nefertiti scoots forward on her platform of blankets and pillows and nests herself between the two front seats. From that point on, the three girls are deep into a conversation about parents.

Nefertiti's not being fair. It's great having a virtual brother! I glance up at Dingus and smile. He smiles back, almost like he knows what I'm thinking.

Dingus pulls the Viarbox gear out of the backpack and helps set it up for Jamie. I catch Dingus' eye, flick a glance toward the front seat and then back to him. *What if Jenny and Amy see the futuristic games?*

Dingus leans forward, peers over Nefertiti's shoulder at the chattering girls, and sits back. He shakes his head and rolls his eyes. *They'll never notice a thing.*

He's right. I shrug and dip my head to the side. *Carry on.*

Dingus nudges Jamie and puts his finger to his mouth, urging him to be quiet as he plays. He tips his chin toward the front seat and, just like that, Jamie is in on our telepathic conspiracy. He nods back at Dingus, indicating he would play the game quietly.

I narrow my eyes in question at Dingus. Dingus silently mouths *Jalopy Junction* in answer. I nod. It's a stupid game - one that comes with the system — but a good choice to ease Jamie into the world of Viarbox and rolling transports.

I watch Jamie's reactions to the game. The boy's initial wide-eyed wonder quickly changes to one of concentration and determination as he plays the game. He looks like he wants to squeal and yell at the other drivers inside the game, but he clenches his mouth, staying silent as promised.

I am impressed with Jamie. I would think such things would terrify a kid from colonial times, but Jamie seems to take it all in with curiosity and excitement.

Still, it's too soon to introduce the boy to something like *Rex*. That was an awesome game that I can't wait to play again. I played *Rex* for the very first time during the tournament – and won.

Or did I win?

I had considered losing the game – and nearly did! If I had lost, I would be off the hook for playing Daemon and Nefertiti would be in my shoes. He's a mean contestant even when he's not mad at you, but at least she isn't on his bad side. The more I think about it, the more I wish I had lost the game.

What a coward I was.

If Daemon hadn't sent us back in time, the tournament would be long over.

What would my life be like now? I imagine the outcome of my final match with Daemon. All I can see is the worst possible scenario. Daemon beats me to a pulp and I spend the rest of the summer in a hospital bed sucking food through a tube. And when school starts again, I'll be the laughing stock of the year. I already have no friends except Dingus. But at least the other kids ignore me. They don't taunt me.

Then I'll be forced to crawl into a dark hole – or a Viarbox game – and spend the rest of my life as a hermit.

That's what my future holds if I return to 2076.

Here in 1976, maybe I can go to Los Angeles and seek my fortune like Jenny and Amy. Jamie doesn't want to go home. Why should I?

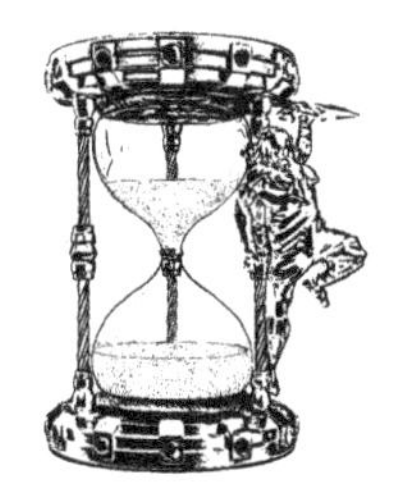

The first kid to climb Mount Everest

Darkness falls by the time we cross into Indiana. Jenny and Amy are yawning and I curse myself for not having the foresight to snooze before now. I can refresh Dingus from time to time to keep him awake indefinitely, but his head disappeared a few minutes ago. It happened fast and no one else saw it, but I can't be sure it won't happen again. We won't get to California very fast with a headless driver.

There's no help for it. I'll have to drive. "Jenny, how about if Nefertiti and I take over driving for the night?"

"Okay," Jenny says willingly in the middle of another yawn. "It's dark so the cops won't notice how young you are."

"No offense, but, are you sure you can drive?" Amy asks.

"I can drive," I say, not offended. A kid who can drive seems to be a novelty to these primitive people.

We do what Jenny calls a *fire drill*. We pull over and everyone gets out of the transport, runs around it and hops back in but in different seats. Nefertiti gets in the front passenger seat. Jenny and Amy climb in the back. Dingus and Jamie are right back where they started. And I hoist myself up into the drivers' seat.

Then, something that never happens in a Viarbox game occurs. My feet don't reach the pedals. I close my eyes, feeling a blush rise up on my cheeks. This is just plain embarrassing. How can I solve this problem without letting everyone in the transport know?

"Hey, technoid," Nefertiti calls back to Dingus. "Nik's too short. Do you think you can rig something?"

I squeeze my eyes tighter. My cheeks flare with heat.

Dingus shrugs confidently, takes the flashlight out of the backpack, and gets out of the transport. While Dingus hunts around the nearby wooded area, I distract Jenny and Amy in case Dingus comes up with some oddly futuristic solution.

Dingus cuts a thick tree branch into blocks using a tool he digs out of his pocket. He then uses wire to secure one block to each of the pedals so I can reach them.

With the problem solved, we are back in our seats and I ease onto the road. It takes me a few minutes to get used to the controls and remember how to drive a transport from this time. I push the transport to go faster, but it's still slower than the maximum speed on the gage.

Everyone in the back of the transport sleeps while I drive. I glance in the rear view mirror. "Ratz. Dingus needs a reboot."

"Leave him go," Nefertiti whispers from her seat beside me. "You can reboot him later before the others wake up."

She's right. "Do you still hate him?" I can't help asking.

I can see Nefertiti's shoulder lift and fall from the corner of my eye. "I don't hate him," she says, "but… I mean… how can a veeb be your best friend? Veebs don't have feelings."

"Are you kidding? Dingus does." But then I add less confidently, "I think he does. He seems to."

"He was just programmed to seem like it, Nikola. He doesn't really *feel* the way humans do."

I feel like a traitor thinking anything less. I glance into the mirror at my frozen friend. "Maybe your virtual mom isn't programmed the same way, but you shouldn't lump all virtual beings into the same category. I wouldn't want Kluge for a friend either. He's as stupid as they come and will do whatever Daemon tells him to do."

"That's the way my virtual mom is. Stupid, but obedient."

Maybe Dingus is different from other virtual beings. They are fairly new. I don't know many on a personal basis to judge the matter. "Dingus is smart. But he's not… obedient. I mean, he makes up his own mind about stuff."

"It doesn't matter anyway," Nefertiti continues. "There's no love lost between us. Dingus growls at me whenever you're out of earshot."

"Are you tattling on Dingus?"

"No! Forget it." Nefertiti crosses her arms and huffs out her nose. "Just forget it!"

"I'm sorry Nefertiti. I didn't… Do you want me to say something to him?"

She doesn't answer.

The lines in the roadway go by as I push the limits of the transport's speed capabilities. No wonder we went so slow. I realize the transport isn't capable of going faster, despite the number eighty on the gage.

"Nefertiti, I think Dingus is just jealous. He's not used to me having another friend. Give him time."

I look over just in time to see a tear slip down her cheek, but she quickly turns away. She remains as frozen as Dingus, with her arms crossed staring out the window.

I realize I had called her a friend. Maybe she's just as lonely as me. Maybe she's vying for my friendship as much as Dingus is fighting to protect it. It's a novelty to me.

Eventually, Nefertiti falls asleep. I keep my foot heavy on the gas and don't let up. I occupy my mind by thinking what it would be like to live the rest of my life in this time.

I could go to Los Angeles and maybe become a star, like Jenny and Amy. Except I can't sing. Or dance. Or act.

I can play Viarbox. But, they don't have Viarbox in this time. Maybe I can go to Indianapolis and become a real race car driver. I'm good at that. Or I can become the first kid to climb Mount Everest. I can get sponsors and be rich.

I wouldn't need school. I wouldn't need to get a job.

I wouldn't need friends.

Would I?

Sometime during the night, somewhere in Illinois, the dark monotony of the road begins to lull me into drowsiness. My only company over the past few hours is a lonely helicopter that flies high in the sky and far behind us, but seems to be traveling in the same direction.

Nefertiti has had several hours of sleep, so I find a gas station with a vending machine. I wake her up and buy her a soda to help her stay awake. We switch places after removing the blocks from the pedals. She doesn't need them.

"Keep the pedal all the way down," I tell her. Then I yawn and am asleep before we leave the parking lot.

I wake up Friday morning to the sound of whispers. It's light outside and I'm still in the front passenger seat of the VW transport. My pocket pilot lay on the center console. Twisting around, I see that Dingus is awake. I catch Nefertiti's gaze and realize she is the one who rebooted him, probably before the others woke up.

Thanks, I mouth to her and smile. She nods and a corner of her mouth lifts.

Nefertiti slows the van into a gas station. Perfect. My neck and legs are stiff and I need to stretch. I also have to use a sanitation room, real bad.

Feeling awake after a stretch, a brisk walk, and a peek at a map, I walk to the picnic table where the others have congregated. Jenny passes around a large bag of chips, Amy offers me a peanut butter cracker from a small pack, and Nefertiti hands me a Coke in a thick glass bottle.

I look at the bottle. The cap is still on and, based on our experiences in Philadelphia, you need the metal thing attached to the machine to open it. Since the machine is twenty feet away, I look up from the useless bottle to address the group. "We're in Missouri."

No one responds.

Jenny tosses me a flat metal tool. "Church key," she says.

I hold the object up and squint at it. It doesn't look like a key no matter what kind of church. Dingus snatches it from my hand and uses it to open my Coke.

I peer into the now open bottle, then take a swig and cough as it both refreshes and burns its way to my empty stomach. I blink and look up at the group again. "I said, we're in *Missouri*!"

"We know," Nefertiti says.

"And?"

"And what?" she says. "We're in Missouri."

"According to the map, we're *barely* in Missouri. Shouldn't we be further than that?"

"Don't get your panties in a wad," Jenny says. "We're making great time."

Dingus smirks at me. *Touché*.

"Besides," Nefertiti says, "We have a bigger problem. I think we're being followed."

"What? By whom? How do you know?"

"A helicopter was right behind us the whole time I was driving."

"Yeah, I've seen it." I tilt my head back and look at the early morning sky in all directions. There's a lonely vapor trail from a faraway jet, but no helicopter. I still can't get over how empty the skyway is in this time. "I don't see it now. Maybe it passed us when we pulled over. It's just going the same way we are."

"No," Nefertiti says. "Helicopters can go much faster than these primitive transports. At least that's what Dingus said. If the helicopter can go so fast, why would the driver choose to stay behind us for that long? I think he's following us."

She has a point. If *any* vehicle could go faster, why would it choose to go slow? "Wait!" I say. "The speed limit, that's why. Even if we can go faster, we have to obey the speed limit so we don't get pulled over. Look how slow that got us. The helicopter was doing the same thing."

"Speed limits don't apply in the sky," Jenny says. "And what do you mean by primitive?"

My eye sprang open at the first thing Jenny said. Dingus and Nefertiti might be right. Could the helicopter really be the agent following us? How could he know where we are?

"Care to tell us why a chopper might be following you?" Jenny asks. She and Amy exchange concerned looks.

Dingus, Nefertiti and I exchange guilty looks.

"Look," Jenny says. "I can dig it. I'm not a narc or anything, but it's not my bag. Amy and I might not want to get mixed up in something bogus. We need to know what it is."

I shake my head. "We can't tell you. I mean, we *can* tell you, but we choose not to." I glance up at Nefertiti and Dingus to make sure they don't contradict me. They both nod. I turn to look at Jenny. "It's not bad, I promise. We're just trying to help someone…well… two people."

"Three," Nefertiti corrects me. "Don't forget Benny."

"Four," Dingus offers. "Don't forget Jamie."

"Okay." Jenny holds her hands up in surrender. "So you're do-gooders on some kind of mission. Why would someone be following you?" She looks at Jamie. "Is this some kind of international espionage or something?"

I shake my head again. "No, nothing like that." At least I hope it isn't *espionage*. I don't know what that means. But Pheloni is an FBI agent, so maybe. He found us in Philadelphia. But, the newspaper article about crashing the plane gave us away. He would have no way of knowing where we are now. I'm sure of that.

"No," I say. "It's nobody. We're fine."

Jenny looks skeptical, but she seems to let it go. We finish our snack, take a brisk walk around the parking lot to loosen sore muscles and pile back into the transport with Amy in the driver's seat.

Morning turns to afternoon, and the sun grows hotter as we slowly plod along south and west. With no air conditioning in the van, we drive with the windows open. The air thunders through the transport, making it too loud for conversation. The girls and Jamie ponytail their hair to keep it from flying into their faces from the wind.

We gas up and eat when needed. I pay for gas twice using the virtual money. And I push to get everyone back in the transport and on the road quickly each time. Afternoon has long since turned into evening. My watch almost seems to be speeding ahead while the transport seems to be driving backward.

Around midnight, the air is cool and the windows are up. Nefertiti is driving.

And the engine dies.

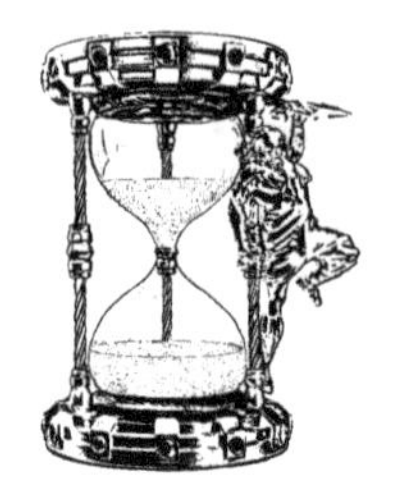

If I could save time in a bottle

Nefertiti struggles to pull over. Even in the darkness, I can see a trail of smoke coming out the back of the van.

Nefertiti turns the motor off and hops out onto the side of the road. Jenny gets in the driver's seat and tries to start it up. It makes a clicking noise, but doesn't start.

"Oh no," Jenny says with a groan. "I had a feeling the engine would tank."

"What?" I say. "When were you going to tell us about this feeling?"

"This boat's been taking a licking but it can't keep ticking forever. We'll have to find a grease monkey in the morning to fix it." Jenny pats the dashboard like she was tucking a child into bed for the night.

I groan.

Everyone climbs out of the transport into the cool night air. We are somewhere just inside northern Texas. It has been dark for a couple hours and I can't tell if we're near anything helpful. I scan the blackness of the night and see nothing. No lights of a town. No headlights from other transports. No moon. Not even the helicopter.

I go back to the transport and dig out my backpack. I root inside it and pull out the flashlight. "C'mon," I say quietly to everyone. I throw the backpack onto my shoulder and start walking down the road.

"Where are you going?" Nefertiti asks.

"There's gotta be a town somewhere. We passed one half an hour ago. There must be another one soon."

Nefertiti and Dingus catch up with me. I keep walking. Nefertiti falls into step on one side while Dingus flanks me on the other side.

"You're not going to walk in the middle of the night to get help." She says it in a way that brooks no arguments.

"Yes, I am," I argue.

"No, you're not," Dingus says on my other side.

I keep walking.

"Nik, this is insane. You don't know how far it is, or what wild animals are out there in the dark. What if a transport comes along? We should stay together."

I don't stop.

"Nik, stop!" She grabs my sleeve and forces me to a stop.

I round on her. "We're behind schedule." I nearly shout. "By a lot! Do you know how slow that transport goes? We cannot just sit by the side of the road and wait until morning. We absolutely must be in California by tomorrow and it took us nearly two days to get this far."

"It'll be okay," Dingus says.

"Yeah, let's wait for a transport to come along," Nefertiti says.

"*You* wait for a transport to come along!" I start walking again. In all honesty, I need to walk after sitting for so long. It helps to keep the tension I feel at bay. Between the slow travel and… I don't want to think about the rest of my stress.

"You can't be slow in beat-the-clock games," I continue, sensing Nefertiti beside me again. "When something happens, you have to keep going. You can't throw in the towel. If I stop every time

Viarbox throws me a curve, I'd never do half the things I've done. We can do this. We can make it to California on time. We can make it to Chicago, too. But, only if we don't stop!"

Nefertiti grabs my sleeve and makes me stop. She faces me and puts her hands on either side of my face. She tips my head up so I can see her face.

"This. Is. Not. A. Game!" she says.

"Yes. It. Is!" I yank myself out of her grasp and step back. "It's always a game. Everything is a game."

I feel Dingus' hand on my shoulder. "It f…f…feels like a game, buddy. But it's n..n…not. Not this time." Dingus slips the backpack off my shoulder and hoists it onto his own. But the pack falls to the ground with a clatter when his arm disappears.

I bend to pick up the pack and lift it back onto my shoulder. "Go back and sit down before your legs fall off, Ding."

"It just seems like a g…g…game," Dingus says, not going back.

"Why does it have to be a game?" Nefertiti asks softly.

"Because in a game…" I stop myself. I almost said that in a game, friends don't matter. Big kids who threatened little kids don't matter.

Life doesn't matter.

"Because in a game, what?" Nefertiti presses.

"Nothing." I start walking again. Now I'm just angry. I don't want my mind to go to some dark place. I just want to keep my mind on the game. I wipe the moisture that begins pooling at the corners of my eyes and then mask the motion by scratching my ear.

"I've decided to stay." I continue walking. I swing the flashlight back and forth ahead of me to watch where I step.

"Then where are you going?" Dingus asks. "The transport's back that way."

"No, yoctobrain. I mean, I've decided to *stay*." I emphasize the last word. "Here in 1976. Forever."

Nefertiti gasps.

"You c... c... caaaan't," Dingus says. "We have to go back. We all have to go back."

I stop and turn to Dingus. "Why? What does it matter? I like it here. Jamie's not going back. Why should I? I can just stay here with him. With Jenny and Amy."

"We haven't decided what to do with Jamie yet," Nefertiti says.

"I don't want to stay here," Dingus whines.

"You're sick, Dingus. You have to go back with Nefertiti."

"No!" Dingus and Nefertiti both shout at the same time.

"You would send me back with her?" Dingus asks incredulously. "What... But... That's..." Dingus stammers and I know it has nothing to do with his illness. I expected Dingus to fight this. I shouldn't have blurted it out like that. I should have kept my thoughts to myself until Wednesday. Now, it's out.

I feel oddly free, as if a giant weight I didn't notice is lifted from my shoulders. I didn't even make up my mind until I said it out loud. It's like that moment in the *Rex* game when my body just acted on its own and won the game for me.

Winning was not an act of cowardice. It was an act of fate. It was meant to be. I was meant to come back to this time.

I am meant to stay.

I can stay with Jamie. Dingus can't. His sickness is getting worse and it must have to do with the time travel. Nefertiti can take care of him. She needs a friend and Dingus will switch loyalties... eventually... maybe. If he doesn't, he can be programmed to like her. That probably isn't a good solution, but at the moment, I don't care.

I will help them get to California and find the priest. I will even make sure we get back to Chicago and get Benny and the native away from Pheloni. I will help everyone get to the airport on time for the replacement.

But, when the moment arrives, I will not be on my mark.

I give up fighting and follow Nefertiti and Dingus back to the transport. By the time we arrive, Jamie has already taken charge and is setting up camp, complete with a fire circle. The boy is crouched over a pile of twigs and straw, banging two rocks together. They spew sparks, but don't catch anything on fire.

"What are you doing?" Dingus asks.

"Where'd you get the straw?" I ask, shining the flashlight into the strawless green field surrounding us.

Jamie looks up at Dingus and then at me. He answers me first. "From me pocket, o' course. I always carry a fire kit. Don't ye?" Then he turns to Dingus. "Sometimes it takes a wee while to ketch."

"Will this help?" Jenny holds up a small shiny metal case. She opens the lid and flicks her thumb across the top. Jamie jumps back when the flame appears. In less than a minute, everyone is feeding sticks to build up the fledgling campfire.

Amy brings the *coup de gras* from a cooler inside the transport — marshmallows! She also has chocolate bars and graham crackers and says we'll make *s'mores*. We have to hunt for sticks to roast the marshmallows. I find one with two prongs on the end. *Righteous*!

It's a delicious treat. I'm sure Dingus is going to regret not indulging in this one for the rest of his life! Instead, Dingus seems content to keep the fire going, stirring the ashes with his stick instead of roasting marshmallows on it.

Amy retrieves her guitar and tambourine from the transport and the girls begin to sing. They have nice voices. And it makes for nice background music. But after the snack, I decide to turn in for the night.

The girls only have two pillows in the transport, but they have quite a few blankets and quilts. Jamie and I spread a thick quilt on the ground on the other side of the fire. This will be the boys' side. A second quilt on top will keep us warm.

For now, I cross my legs on the edge of the quilt and watch the flames of the campfire dance to the flow of the music. Dingus throws another thick branch on the fire and sends a spray of sparks into the air like fireworks.

The girls sing about saving time in a bottle. I snort and wonder how I might use the time travel program to my advantage against Daemon. If the program always returns me to the same moment, how can I ever escape Daemon unless I stay in the past? Is that the same thing as saving time in a bottle?

And what use is a time travel program if nothing changes? I either have to jump over time and get to the other side of the tournament, or stay on this side, safe and sound in 1976. I just want to bottle up the middle part where I have to face Daemon. Then I would hide the bottle and never tell anyone where it is.

If only I could keep Dingus with me.

As the girls sing, Jamie teaches me the finer points of flinging a marble with speed and accuracy. I try to hit the other marble directly on with enough force to knock it out of the circle. Jamie is quite good at it. I am getting better.

After a while, Jamie collects his marbles and I lay back on the quilt. A chorus of chirping crickets sing along with the girls.

Dingus crawls one-legged over to me and stretches out. I glance across the fire, but the girls are busy singing. I pull the second quilt over where Dingus' legs should be. Jamie stretches out on my other side.

We lay in a row on our backs, with our hands cupped behind our heads while the girls' sing about wishing on a star. I look up to find a star to wish upon, but can't decide which one. There seems to be more in this time. At least you can be sure they're stars because they stay still.

"What happened to all the stars?" Jamie asks, eerily touching on the opposite of my thought. "Have they gone away?"

"Artificial lights in the big cities," Dingus says. "The stars are there. You just can't see them because it's too bright on earth. It's even worse in our time. You're not really going to stay are you?" Dingus directs the last to me.

"No." I lie. There's no point upsetting Dingus until the time comes for him to go. "I'm just grumpy. Don't mind me."

The girls continue to sing. The crickets continue to chirp. The stars continue to twinkle. And I drift off to sleep.

I awake Saturday morning to the roar of an engine. Sitting up, I rub my eyes against the brightness of the morning. I see Dingus, all arms and legs in working order, bent over the back of the VW transport. Nefertiti hovers over Dingus as if supervising him and Jenny is in the drivers' seat.

"Sounds primo!" Jenny calls to Dingus. "What did you do?"

"Just gave it a little tweak." Dingus looks over at me. "Good morning. You coming, or what?"

I jump to my feet. Everyone else is awake and have cleaned up camp. All that's left to do is gather the blanket beneath me.

"Good as new!" Dingus slams shut the back of the transport. He and Nefertiti share a high five.

"Since when…" I am about to ask Dingus and Nefertiti since when are they not completely repulsed by each other, but the sound of a siren floats on the air. I look down the roadway in the direction of the sound and watch until I see a flashing blue light in the distance.

"Oh no!" Something bangs inside my chest.

"Cops!" Amy says.

"Everybody in the transport!" Dingus scrambles into the driver's seat. Jenny helps toss their belongings in the side door and ushers everyone inside. I jump in the front seat next to Dingus and adjust the mirror outside my window so I can see what's happening.

The approaching transport comes to a stop behind us. Instead of a police vehicle, it's a regular transport with a blue light on top. The door opens and a man steps out. Pheloni!

"Turn off the engine and get out of the vehicle," he calls to us. He draws his gun.

I feel myself thrown back into my seat as Dingus steps on the gas. The transport kicks up dirt and stones and literally leaves Pheloni in the dust. He jumps back into his car. Our transport jolts a second time and I am sucked deeper into my seat. Pheloni's transport falls far behind and is out of sight in a very short time.

My heart is racing. This is the fastest we've moved since Philadelphia. The speed gage is way past the eighty mark.

"What did you do, Dingus?" I want to punch him for not doing it sooner, but I'm too glad to be moving at a respectable speed.

"I fixed the engine." Dingus waggles his eyebrows. A chorus of exclamations came from the backseat.

"Far out!"

"I didn't know this thing could move so fast."

"Ohmagod!"

"Woah!"

"Yahooo!" I punch the air, but hit the ceiling. I grin as I rub my knuckles.

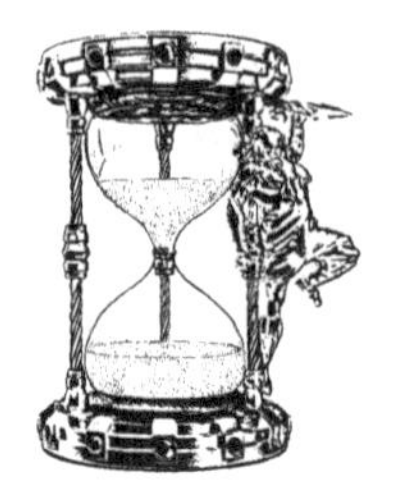

Sanctuary at the old mission

By two o'clock Saturday afternoon, our VW transport rolls into San Diego. It took only eight hours since we left our camp in Texas – a feat that Jenny assures me is impossible.

Dingus had driven most of the way. The first time his right leg disappeared, with a sudden reduction in speed in the middle of the Arizona desert, he simply pulled an impossibly long metal rod out of the deep recesses of his pocket and used it to keep pressure on the gas pedal. Luckily, the girls hadn't noticed any of it. Dingus kept the rod by his side the rest of the journey. His head, thankfully, remained firmly on his shoulders for the entire ride.

I am thrilled to finally be making progress. "Find the white church that was built in 1776." I tell Dingus.

Dingus nods. His internal navigation is newer than these roads and at one point, he takes us to a dead end. But he doubles back and tries another route. Eventually we come to the San Diego de Alcalá mission. On the parking lot, everyone practically falls out of the transport and stands on stiff legs and sore muscles.

"Where are we?" Jenny asks. "What is this place?"

"This is our destination," I say. "Uh... thank you for the ride. We're here now."

Jenny narrows her eyes at me. "What do you mean? That's it? We're here, you can go now?"

I feel my cheeks heat up. I'm not good at this. "Well..."

"What Nikola means," Nefertiti interrupts, "is that now we're here. Let's go inside." She turns to me. "Isn't that what you meant to say to your new *friends*?"

Friends.

I glance at Dingus, who gives a barely perceptible shoulder shrug.

"Yeah, that's what I meant. Um, we should go inside," I say to Jenny.

After climbing the steep steps and through the tall iron visitor's gate, the six of us line up in front of the mission gift shop. A woman assures us we cannot see the priest at this time, but invites us back for Mass at 5:00. We can speak with him afterward.

The woman does not seem to know about *our* priest. She apparently refers to the church's regular priest.

I am sure the priest from 1776 is somewhere close by. Even Jamie, who takes easily to the time shift and finds everything to be amazing, still stuck to familiar grounds in the Philadelphia's Old City. If Jamie had wandered outside that area, we never would have found him. The priest was in the midst of constructing this very building at the time of his displacement. Surely, he would not wander off.

He has to be here. He just has to!

With no recourse but to wait for the church service, we walk companionably down the road until we find a sandwich shop. Inside, we pull extra chairs up to fit around a single table.

I thumb through our depleting virtual funds to make sure we can spare enough for at least three burgers. I consider paying for all of us as a way of thanking Jenny and Amy, but I don't know what lay ahead and hesitate to offer. Dingus, who is whole at the moment, costs nothing whether he eats or not.

Jenny must have caught my hesitation over my open wallet and offers to split the cost evenly. That's more than fair since, if you count Dingus, which I don't but Jenny does, there are four of us and only two of them. But I convince her to order five burgers and two plates of fries to share. We also order two large drinks.

"Now, then," says Jenny, bringing the meeting to order while we wait for our food. "What's next on the agenda, now that you've arrived at your destination?"

"Well, er…" I glance at Nefertiti and Dingus.

"We are here to rescue the priest," Jamie supplies, helpfully.

"Rescue?" Amy says.

"Ah… heh heh…" I pat Jamie's arm. "Sort of. He's not in any danger. We just have to give him a message. After that's done, we have to go to Chicago."

"To rescue the red Indian," Jamie says.

"Red Indian?" asks Amy.

"Chicago?" asks Jenny. "So this isn't your final destination?"

I start to answer but Dingus' head decides to vanish.

Jenny screams. Amy scrapes her chair backward as if to get away. Nefertiti and I jump out of our seats and nearly crash into each other in our hurry to block Dingus from view.

When Dingus' head reappears and seems stable, Nefertiti and I take our seats.

"Wha…" says Amy, wide eyed. She hesitates and then steps toward the table.

"Dingus is vee… vee urtual," Jamie explains. 'Tis queer that, but he willna hurt ye, aye."

Dingus gives me an apologetic look.

"We better explain," Nefertiti says.

I was hoping to ditch the girls before explanations became necessary. We managed to hide Dingus' illness from the girls for the past two days and now, just when we could have… well… it's too late for what ifs. I glare at Nefertiti, but then nod to let her do the talking.

Jenny and Amy, mouths open, stare at the four of us, from one to the next as Nefertiti talks. She explains not only Dingus but everything, just as we had explained to Jamie and Benny.

Amy swallows. "Faaar out." The waitress brings our burgers and Nefertiti mumbles a thank you. No one touches the food. Jenny reaches out and pokes Dingus in the arm.

"Ow!" Dingus grabs his arm. "Why is that the first thing everyone does to me?"

"He feels real to me," Jenny says.

"Of course I do!"

After a minute of silence, Jenny picks up her burger. "So, we're going to Chicago. I can live with that." She takes a bite.

"No, *we're* going to Chicago," I correct.

Jenny chews and then swallows. "Oh? And how are *you* going to get there?"

"We… I mean…"

"Oh, give it up, Nik." Nefertiti turns to Jenny. "Of course you can come with us." The girls, who are now apparently best friends, hug each other.

I try one more time. "Once we finish up in Chicago, we're going home to our own time." I look guiltily at Dingus, who raises an eyebrow. *Are you?*

I look away, not wanting to lie to Dingus again. I consider Jenny's question. Jenny and Amy now know the truth about us. Keeping them close means less risk of even more people finding out. And they do have a transport that can go one hundred and fifty miles per hour. Once Nefertiti and Dingus go back to 2076, I can return to Los Angeles with Jamie, Jenny and Amy. *If only Dingus could stay, too.*

"Okay. You can come" I say to Jenny. I glance at Dingus, who nods. Then Dingus' arm disappears.

"Far out."

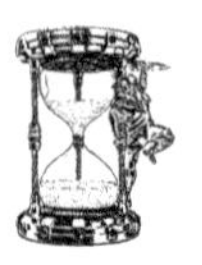

Not having a clue what to do at a Catholic Mass, I follow Amy's lead as she enters the church, kneels, touches her head and shoulders, and then sits in a pew. Through the service, I do everything she does, except sing. As expected, the priest conducting the service is not the one we're looking for, nor do I see any sign of him within the church. Nefertiti lays a hand on my fidgety leg and squeezes. I sit through the rest of the service trying to be still.

After the service all the people get up to leave. I remain seated, facing front, to watch the priest. When he goes through a private door at the side of the altar, I burst out of my pew and run to the front of the church, up the steps, across the floor to the little door. I look back and my comrades all look stunned at my sudden action. But they remain sitting. I gesture with my hand for them to stay there and then turn to push the door open.

The priest is hanging up the robe he had worn over his clothing. He looks up and sees me. His features change fluidly from wide-eyed surprise, to narrow-eyed anger to tilt-headed curiosity. "Are you lost, son? This is a private chamber," he says in a calm voice.

"I… I'm looking for a priest."

He smiles. "It seems you've come to the right place. You can call me Pastor Bob. If you wait in the church, I'll join you in a few minutes."

"No… er, I mean… Thank you, but… I mean… I'm looking for a different priest."

"Ah! I'm just a visiting Priest. The regular priest here is away for a few weeks."

"No, not him either."

Pastor Bob's smile falls.

"A priest who came here about a week ago," I explain. "He might have been confused or disoriented."

Pastor Bob's eyes light up for the barest second before taking on a blank expression. "I cannot say…"

"Yes, you can! I've come a long way to find him. I… we're here to help him."

He looks over my shoulder and back. "We?"

"Me and… my… associates."

He shakes his head. "I'm sorry, son. I don't… There's no one here by that description. Now, please…" he strides past me and opens the door.

"You know something, don't you?"

The priest doesn't answer. He just holds the door open.

"Please, talk to us. We'll wait in the church for you, okay?"

Pastor Bob doesn't even look at me now. I drop my head and shuffle my feet to the door. If the colonial priest isn't here, where else could he be? Pastor Bob has to be lying. I saw it in his eyes. Where else would the colonial priest possibly go? He would have been afraid and this would be a familiar place. Just like Jamie. Unless he said something that made people think he was insane. Maybe they locked him up somewhere.

I plop down in a pew.

"Well?" Nefertiti stands over me with hands on her hips. Everyone else is looking expectantly at me too.

"He denies that the colonial priest is here, but I saw recognition in his face when I mentioned him. Either he's lying… or maybe the colonial priest was here and now isn't. But I'm sure he at least *was* here."

Nefertiti sits in the pew beside me. "Of course he was here. If he left, we have to find out where he went. You have to talk to that priest again."

I look toward the private door and see Pastor Bob lean out of the room. When my eyes meet his, he pulls his head back into the room and shuts the door.

"I told him we'd wait here to talk to him after he gets changed." Maybe I just surprised him when I barged into his private chamber. Maybe he was just off balance. I settle into the pew to wait.

A half hour later, we are still waiting.

"Let's have a look around the grounds," Jenny suggests. "If that priest is lying, maybe we'll find a clue to the other."

"A priest would not lie," Amy says defensively.

I am, of course, game for having a look around. We can't risk not looking, so I follow the others out the side door.

The church is also a museum of sorts so we wander the grounds, down the paths of the floral courtyard, through the historic buildings, across the parking lot to the Native American hut display and archeological dig site and back toward the museum. Everyone is busy reading signs and viewing exhibits. I am completely uninterested. I'm not going to find our priest behind the glass covered walls of displayed artifacts.

"Nik, why aren't you reading the displays?" Nefertiti says.

"What's the point?"

"The point..." she grabs my arm and pulls me to one of the displays, "is that you might learn something. Look!"

How can I get excited about learning when I have bigger things to worry about?

"Read it," Nefertiti urges. "It's about a priest named Father Junipero Serra. I think it might be *our* priest. Like he's famous or something. Don't you remember, in the bowl, he was at a construction site? He was at *this* construction site... when this place was being built. Now it's a museum, so of course he would be famous. He built it!"

Suddenly, everything about the place seems interesting and I melt in with the others, eagerly absorbing any information about this priest named Father Serra. If it has someone else's name, I ignore it and move to the next display. There's even a statue of Father Serra in the courtyard. I barely noticed it earlier, but I remember the sense of familiarity when I first saw it. Like I've seen this man before. Of course I have. In the bowl. Yes! Our priest has to be this man.

But, this man is here only as words on a wall. I don't see one sign of him in the flesh. I sit on the bench beside his statue while the others continued to explore. I feel the need to be alone just now. I'm not used to being part of a large group. I think better when I'm alone.

I sit rolling a stone around in circles with my foot, wondering if I should feel defeated. I wonder if we should go search nearby hospitals or mental institutions. I wonder if we should just give up and go to Chicago. Father Serra is in no danger here and maybe, like Jamie, he wants to stay.

On the other hand, not getting Father Serra back will actually change history. He has more of California to settle. We can't let that happen.

A shadow falls on me, but I don't look up. It's just Dingus or one of the others coming to join me on the bench. But, when the person sits beside me, I stiffen and look up at Pastor Bob.

"You and your friends will have to leave soon. We're not really open for tourists at this hour."

"We're not tourists." I cup my hand over my brow to block the brightness of the setting sun. "We're just trying to find Father Ser... I mean... the other priest."

He raises an eyebrow. "Father Ser... What were you about to say?"

"Please..." I say. "Please tell me if you saw him. Even if it sounds strange. If he's somewhere else, I need to find him. But, I don't know where to look. If you know anything..." I stretch my eyes open, hopeful.

"Why is it so important that you find this man?"

"We… we have a message for him."

Pastor Bob looks expectantly, waiting for more information.

"He's not where he belongs," I say. "I mean… he is, but… well… I can't explain, but we just want to help him get back to his ti… home. I know he must be afraid."

Pastor Bob sits in silence for a very long time. I look back to the ground and pick up where I had left off, rolling the rock with my shoe. Eventually Pastor Bob stands up and walks away without another word.

I remain on the bench until the others trickle into the courtyard and join me.

"A woman says we have to leave," Nefertiti informs me. "They aren't open for tourists this late on a Saturday."

I look up and nod. We can come back in the morning for Sunday church service and try again. We make our way through the visitors gate and step out onto the landing at the top of the steps, which overlooks the parking lot.

When I am halfway down the steps I see two other transports on the lot. Four doors open from one vehicle and four men step out. They all turn and watch me descend the stairs.

Pheloni steps out of the second transport.

I stop. The others stop behind me.

"I need all of you to come with me," Pheloni says.

Our previous travel companion, the helicopter, appears out of nowhere in the air above us. Without conscious thought, I turn and race back up the steps. The others follow.

The woman just closed the visitor's gate when I crash into it. "Let us in! Let us in!" She drops a large set of keys and pushes the gate against my efforts to open it. Dingus, Nefertiti, Jamie, Jenny and Amy join in the tug of war and the woman quickly loses the fight. Once we're all through, I bend and scoop up the keys. "Which one?" I shout to the woman. I see Pheloni at the top of the stairs. He rushes toward the gate and slams into it.

Six of us push against Pheloni. Another man comes up behind Pheloni and helps push on the other side. More men reach the top of the steps. Five men against six kids. I don't like our odds.

"The key!" I shout to the woman, whose stunned expression at the scene in front of her tells me she doesn't hear me.

I look at the lock. I look at the keys. I choose the one that looks like it would fit. I stick it in the hole. The key turns.

"You kids are to come with me." Pheloni slams his open palm against the now locked gate.

"What's going on here?" Pastor Bob is suddenly behind me.

"I must take this boy to his mother..."

"He's lying!" I whip around to Pastor Bob. "He wants to hurt us."

"Do you wish to request sanctuary?" Pastor Bob stands with his hands folded in front of him. He calmly looks from me to Dingus to Nefertiti and the others. "All of you?"

"Sanctuary?" I say.

"Don't pull that trick, Padre!" Pheloni says. "It won't work."

"Go get a court order," Pastor Bob says to Pheloni. Then he raises an eyebrow in question to me. "Well?"

I don't know what to say. What does sanctuary mean?

Pastor Bob answers my unspoken question. "There's a room in the church for those claiming sanctuary. It's a very old custom, but it seems to be regaining popularity this week. You may have to share with *someone else...* who is *there,* but..."

Nefertiti gasps behind me. "He's here."

Pastor Bob is now smiling. "Am I to understand you *do* wish to request sanctuary?"

"Yes!" Six voices rise up at once.

"Yes," I repeat. "We wish to request... um... sant,"

"Sanctuary."

"Yeah, that."

"Granted." Pastor Bob turns to the men at the gate. "I'm sorry gentlemen, but these children are now under my protection."

"Oh no you don't. They are to come with me."

Pastor Bob places himself between us and the gate, turns his back on the men, and spreads his arms wide. He shepherds us through the grounds and into the safety of the church.

Just inside the doors, Pastor Bob says to me. "I don't suppose you speak Spanish, do you?"

"He *is* here, isn't he?" I speak with certainty.

Pastor Bob tips his head and lifts a shoulder in mock guilt as if saying, "You caught me." Then he tilts his chin toward the wooden door on the other side of the church. "He's just over there."

I grin at Pastor Bob and hold out my hand to Dingus. "I'm going in, Dingus! I need to speak Spanish."

Dingus reaches into his pocket, pulls out two small, toy-like megaphones, and slaps them into my palm.

Then Dingus' arm disappears. Pastor Bob gasps. I stride toward the door.

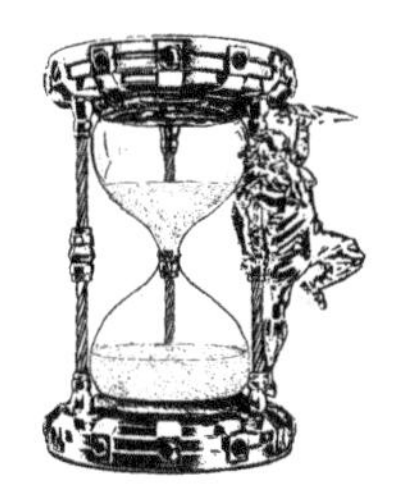

Christopher Columbus of the 21st century

I knock on the wooden door, bouncing on my toes like I'm about to meet the King of England. A contradictory wave of fear and relief sweeps over me.

The door opens and I immediately sense it won't be so bad. Father Serra, not a palace guard, opens the door and waives me in to the small, nearly empty room.

"Entrar, mi hijo."

I don't speak Spanish, but it sounds like an invitation. I step inside. The light bulb overhead is turned off and a candelabra on a sideboard illuminates the room.

Father Serra is not much taller than me. He's wearing a black robe instead of the brown one we saw in the bowl. He probably borrowed it from Pastor Bob. He gestures for me to sit on one side of the wooden table while he sits on the other side. There is a Bible in the center of the table, closed but with a bookmark sticking out of it.

Father Serra neatly folds his hands on the table and studies me as if sizing me up.

I don't want to overstep some religious protocol, so I wait for Father Serra to either speak first or invite me to do so.

"Me han dicho que tienes algo de magia que me puede volver a mi... casa."

I narrow my eyes, not comprehending. "Oh!" I lift one of the megaphones to my mouth, push a button, and say into it, "English to Spanish." Then I hold up the other one and say, "Spanish to English." I hand one to Father Serra. "Take it." Then I remember to hold the translator to my mouth and repeat, "Take it."

Father Serra's eyes spring open. I quickly soothe him, using the translator. "It's okay. It will help us talk and understand each other."

"Ah," Father Serra says.

"Hold it up to your mouth when you speak and I'll understand what you say, just like you can understand me now."

Father Serra squints to study the device. He turns it over in his palm and then over again. Finally, he puts it to his mouth. "You will understand me if I speak into the object?"

"Yes," I say into mine. So far, so good. At least the priest didn't bolt. We can finally get down to business. I nod to Father Serra to restart the conversation.

"You truly do have magic." He gestures to the translator. "I understand you also have magic that can return me home."

"Yes, I do."

Father Serra studies me suspiciously. "From where does this magic come?"

"It's not really magic. It's science."

"I will not allow that which is evil."

"Science isn't evil. It's just... science."

"I do not understand." Father Serra speaks with patience, as if he wants to understand and is waiting for me to explain. But, I don't know how to explain it. People in medieval times were afraid of things they didn't understand. And they generally killed whatever they were afraid of. Father Serra isn't from medieval times, but he isn't that far from it. Did they still burn witches in his time?

The thought gives me an idea. "Do you know that people once thought the Earth was flat and that it was the center of the universe?"

Father Serra smiles. "Yes."

"And what do you think about those people?"

"They did not yet understand the vast power of our Lord," he says.

"Right," I say. "But, during that time, anyone who dared to say the Earth was not the center of the universe was criticized – probably burned at the stake for even thinking it, right?"

Father Serra nods. "Sadly, that is true."

"It's because the people were afraid of anything that wasn't exactly what they grew up knowing. They were afraid of what they didn't understand. They thought if they didn't know about it, then it must be evil. But it wasn't evil. Eventually, everyone knew the earth was round and that it isn't even close to the center of the universe."

Father Serra nods again.

"Science made that discovery. You're not afraid of that are you?"

"No."

"This device you're talking into is just another scientific invention. It's not magic. It's science. It's no more evil than knowing the Earth isn't flat." I wait for him to absorb this bit of information.

At his nod, I continue. "It was also science that brought you to this time. You are from the year 1776." I put my hand on my own chest. "I am from the year 2076. And you and me are both now in the year 1976. Do you understand?"

The father takes a good long time before nodding.

"This science is very new. We are the first people to use it. We're like... like...someone making a new discovery. Like..."

"Christopher Columbus!" Father Serra beams with excitement.

"Yes! We're like Christopher Columbus. We're the first to travel into the unknown."

"Ahh." Father Serra leans back on his chair. "Glory be to God for such gifts!"

"But," I warn with a raised finger. "It's still unknown science in this time and in your own time. You cannot talk about it to anyone."

"People will be afraid of it," Father Serra says.

"Yes. You cannot be famous for it like Christopher Columbus. You have to be famous for other stuff anyway."

Father Serra nods. I assume he has seen the displays about himself.

"You have a device that can send me home?" Father Serra asks.

"Not exactly," I say. "There is a device, but it's in the year 2076." When Father's hopeful expression deflates, I quickly amend. "But, it can still get you home."

"How?"

I explain about the replacement sequence and what he has to do to go home. Adjusting for the time zone differential, I tell him the date and time that he must stand on the exact same spot as when he first arrived. I'm sure Pastor Bob will help once we explain everything. I suspect he will also keep our secret.

Father Serra says he will be pleased to return to the exact same moment of his displacement so no one will worry about his absence. "And you…? Will you return to your time at the same moment?"

I hesitate "Yes…. But we have another person like you to help first."

"Another…"

"There are three like you, actually. We have one with us and we know where to find the other. We just have to get there."

"I see." Father Serra is quiet as he studies me. "You spoke an untruth to me just now."

What? Doesn't he believe my story? "What do you mean?"

"I asked if you will go home when I do. You hesitated. When you answered, your eyes looked away. I think you are not telling the truth."

I cough to mask my surprise. "I… I… I mean,"

"You see? It was a simple question. You need not have been intimidated by it. I have caught you in a lie. Would you care to confess? I am a priest, you know."

"I…"

Father Serra folds his hands on the table again, displaying patience. I look around the room for a distraction but there is no way out of this one. Finally, I sit back and huff.

"I'm not going back. I'm staying here. Well… not here in this church. I mean here in 1976."

"Staying? Are you a missionary, then?"

"Missionary?"

"Have you come to 1976 in order to teach? To save souls?"

"Oh no! Nothing like that. I just don't want to go home."

"But you are an explorer. You are Christopher Columbus from the future. Do you not need to return and deliver your discoveries to your king?"

"No. I don't have a king. I mean… well…"

"Why do you not wish to return?"

"It's like you said. I'm Christopher Columbus. I'll send the others back with the discoveries, but I'll stay here to keep exploring."

"Tsk." Father Serra looks over the bridge of his nose at me.

I look around the room again. I look everywhere but at him.

He leans across the table and delicately holds my chin with his forefinger and thumb. "Look at me," he says into his translator.

I look at him.

"If you cannot tell your priest what troubles you, who can you tell?"

I shake my head to release his touch. The sudden movement jars a tear loose and I feel it slide down my cheek. That threatens to unleash more tears and I clear my throat to prevent it.

"I don't like my time," I say matter-of-factly.

"What do you not like about it?"

A great tug of war ensues while Father Serra extracts my story. I beat around the bush not wanting to talk about it, but I finally give in and tell Father Serra about the tournament and Daemon's threat.

"Besides, it's not like I'm leaving a boatload of friends behind." I hear the sound of my own voice saying those words and immediately wish I hadn't said them. I sound like a real loser.

Father Serra narrows his eyes. "What about the companions who came with you? Are they not your friends?"

"No. Well, one is. I mean two… um… three. Well, maybe, yes. Yes. YES! They are my friends!"

"I thought as much," Father Serra says. "You had said you have been a week on this journey. I myself have journeyed several months at a time on foot into unknown territories. I have met people who frightened me and others who were a curiosity to me. But, many of those whom I've met along the way I now consider to be my friends. I could not have succeeded without them."

I blink as Father Serra studies my face, perhaps waiting for a response. "Ah, but that is life," Father Serra continues. "You meet friends at every turn, do you not?"

"No." I wipe my wet face with my sleeve, finally thinking what I want to say. "You don't understand. I'm just not good at making friends. I'd like to keep Dingus with me, but he's sick and needs to go home. He might even die if he stays. But, I can't go home! Daemon will turn me into a steaming mass of seventh grade pulp — in front of the whole town. The whole state! On live television! He's way bigger than me. He can do it."

Father Serra looks like he's about to speak, but I cut him off. "Look, I really don't want to talk about this anymore, okay?"

"There are two possible solutions to your dilemma," Father Serra offers. "Have you heard the story of David and the Philistine? No?" he says upon seeing my expression. "David was a small boy who had volunteered to fight a mighty warrior whom no one else would dare to challenge. He tried to wear a soldier's armor, but it was too heavy for his small body. So he went in unprotected, save the Lord on his side. He defeated the goliath warrior with nothing but a stone and his sling shot. That boy went on to become a great king."

Father Serra pauses in his tale and looks at me curiously. "Do you know how to use a sling?"

I shake my head.

"Ah, never mind. Then, I think you should try the other tactic. Love your enemies as the Lord has commanded."

I cough to mask my revulsion at the thought. This guy obviously doesn't comprehend the situation.

"Yes, that is the answer," Father Serra continues. "You must attack your enemy by befriending him."

"Befriend… No way," I say.

"As your friend," Father Serra continues as if I hadn't spoken, "he will not strike you, nor any new friends that you acquire."

"That's *never* gonna happen."

"As your friend, he will come to understand you."

"I really, *really* don't want to talk about this anymore. Can we please be done?" I call in reinforcements by pleading with my eyes, begging Father Serra – who is supposed to be a humanitarian – not to force me to talk about this anymore.

Father Serra holds up one hand. "You have told me how to solve my problem. And now, I have told you how to solve yours. You must heed my counsel, as I will yours." He sets the translating device on the table, folds his hands across his belly, and leans back on the chair.

I assume that means I'm dismissed. *Good.* I scoop up his translator and can't get out of there fast enough. Before leaving, I turn back to Father Serra, holding the translator to my mouth. "Do you remember the exact location of your displacement?"

Father Serra nods.

"Good." I step out of the room and pull the door closed. Mission accomplished.

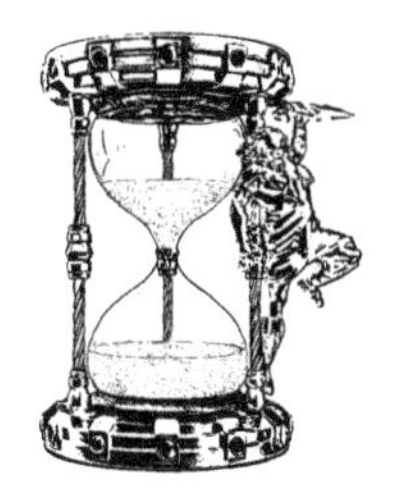

A friend's sacrifice

Having delivered the message to Father Serra, I preside over the largest dump-out-the-pack session ever. Jenny and Amy are now in on the game – or 'not-a-game' as Nefertiti reminds me.

We sit in a circle on the floor of the church. I explain how the game/not-a-game works to Jenny and Amy. I know dumping out the pack is useless, but it's ceremonial at this point and it does make everyone's minds focus on this one task.

It is time to move on to Chicago. But how? The place is surrounded with FBI or cops or Pheloni's henchmen - or whatever they are. Well, maybe 'surrounded' is a little overly dramatic. Still, five men and a helicopter have us trapped.

Unless… I wonder if getting caught will get us transported to Chicago in a hurry. But, we'd have to break ourselves out of prison, or wherever Pheloni intends to put us, before we can even think of rescuing Benny and the native. *Is Dingus right about the use of torture in this time?*

The speed of transportation might not outweigh the consequences. We need to get to Chicago under our own terms.

"A diversion." Dingus breaks into my thoughts, already ahead of me.

I raise an eyebrow for Dingus to continue.

"It'll be dark soon. They may be off guard or at least getting bored. Jenny, Amy and I can sneak out to the transport and pretend to be getting away. We'll let them chase us. Meanwhile, you, Nefertiti and Jamie can slip out and get away. I'll disappear once I'm out of range of your pocket pilot and you can click me back to wherever you are."

"But, they'll capture Jenny and Amy," I say. "We'd have to rescue them."

"Don't worry about us," Jenny says. "Your agent doesn't need us for anything. They'll either release us, or turn us over to real police who will send us home."

"But, you're running away," Nefertiti says. "Why would you want to go home?"

Jenny looks at Nefertiti and then to Amy. She lifts one shoulder and lets it fall "I'll be eighteen soon enough. So will Amy. Besides, our home life isn't as bad as we made it sound. As much as I want to continue this adventure, I think going home will help you more."

I swallow my retort. That is probably the most generous thing anyone has ever done for me. These girls, who hardly know me, are sacrificing themselves for me. Well… I tell myself they're doing it for Nefertiti.

I stand up and go to the door at the back of the church. I line my eyeball up to the crack between the doors, but I can't get a good view of the parking lot or the men on it. I need to get up higher. I can go out to the courtyard and up the steps to peek through the open design of the clay structure where the bells hang. But, the outside courtyard is visible from the air. I'll have to wait for full darkness.

Maybe this idea of Dingus' will work. There are lots of places to sneak onto the parking lot. If Dingus and the girls can make it to the transport, it just might work.

Darkness covers the grounds quickly. Only a single street light sheds a weak light on the parking lot. I spy from the cutouts in the clay wall where the bells hang, and watch Dingus, Jenny and Amy stealthily make their way to Jenny's transport.

Jenny's and one other transport are the only ones on the lot. Pheloni's transport is gone. It is something of a miracle that the men don't see the three kids ducking past them in the shadow.

Then Jenny starts the engine and four doors open on the other transport.

Jenny backs out of her space and floors it out of the parking lot. The four doors quickly close and the transport follows in Jenny's wake.

The helicopter turns the spotlight on to the empty parking lot and moves it across the asphalt and surrounding area. Then it shines on the perimeter of the church as if checking for movement. Finally, the helicopter blasts its light into the courtyard. I tuck my legs up inside the cutout. Jamie and Nefertiti are inside the church door.

I impatiently wait with my knees tucked up to my chin for the helicopter to join the chase. Every minute delays our real escape. After several minutes, the helicopter finally flies off in the direction Jenny went. I waste no time rounding up Nefertiti and Jamie.

Back inside the church, we cross the pews toward the exit door on the opposite side. Then I see both priests at the top of the altar steps. I motion for Nefertiti and Jamie to wait and I run up the steps to the two priests.

"Thanks," I say. "I mean, for your help." I turn to Father Serra. "Gracias." I don't have the translator and that's all I know how to say.

Father Serra nods.

"Go with God," Pastor Bob says.

I nod and spin around to Nefertiti and Jamie. The side door leads to a rear parking lot. Nefertiti, Jamie and I dash across the lot and climb over the fence. I breath heavily as I trudge up the steep hill. Wordlessly, the three of us go higher and higher. Leaves crunch under our feet.

At the top of the hill, I have a good view and a better sense of which way to go. East seems the obvious direction because it's away from danger. But we need to go toward potential transportation. Any crowded area will be even better than that.

I see the helicopter in the distance and know which way the VW transport has gone. We head in the same direction.

"What are you doing?" Nefertiti says. "We want to go that way!" She point behind us.

"Yeah, I know. But, once they discover we're not in the transport with the others, they'll come back for us. They'll know we escaped and that's the direction they'll assume we went."

"Ha!" Jamie says. "I did the same one time. It worked verra weel, aye."

Nefertiti doesn't respond, which I take to mean she agrees.

The helicopter hovers about a mile away. I'm sure that means Pheloni's cohorts have caught the girls' transport. If they were in the desert, that wouldn't have happened. But they're not in the desert.

We race along the hillside ridge, hidden by the foliage. I don't click Dingus back to me for two reasons. One, Dingus will slow us down. Two, if we can't have Dingus for this part of our escape, at least Jenny and Amy can.

But once we get past Dingus' two-mile range, he will simply blink out. And, as long as he doesn't blink out, he'll know that we are closing the distance. I hope that Dingus is smart enough to figure all that out. It seems like a scheme he would come up with himself, and that gives me confidence.

We make our way toward the helicopter. Eventually, we're close enough to see flashing lights on the highway. We watch the scene unfold from our vantage point on the hillside above the highway.

A second transport, a real police car, shows up. That might work in our favor. The helicopter flies back to the mission and circles it slowly, searching – and then heads exactly in the direction I expected them to go.

"What are they doing?" Nefertiti whispers, gesturing to the scene on the highway.

"I don't know," I say.

"They've dumped the pack for the game," Jamie says.

"I don't think so," I say. "They're not part of our game."

Two men have dumped Amy's purse on the hood of their transport and are rummaging through it. The real police put Dingus and the two girls in the backseat of the police transport and then talk to Pheloni's henchmen. They have a discussion and flash each other badges or identification. Eventually two of the four henchmen scoop everything back into Amy's bag and hand it to a police officer.

The police car leaves the scene with Dingus and the girls. *Perfect.*

When the henchmen are in their own transports, they drive away, leaving Jenny's transport by the side of the road.

I click my pocket pilot twice.

"Are you crazy?" Dingus scolds, when he appears by my side. "Put me back. They'll notice I'm gone."

"What were they doing with Jenny's bag?" I ask unperturbed.

"Looking for the keys to the transport." Dingus smiles and waggles his eyebrows.

"You've got them don't you?" I already know the answer before Dingus pats his pocket.

"Jenny was right," Dingus says. "The real police showed up and Pheloni's men had no choice but to let them take us. Now, put me back in the police transport before they get too far away. Then wait about ten minutes. They'll think I escaped. If they notice I'm gone now, they'll search the area, but we're too close to the transport. Jenny said to take it if we can."

I click the undo button to return him to the police transport. Then Nefertiti, Jamie and I make our way down the hillside. We crouch beside a bush to finish our ten-minute wait. When I click Dingus back to me he smiles. "Perfect timing. We were just put in a private room."

We approach Jenny's transport. An occasional car speeds past it, but no one is around. I check one more time for the helicopter. It is a mile away over the mission.

Dingus unlocks the transport, but insists Nefertiti drive. We have no time to attach the blocks for me to reach the pedals and can't risk parts of Dingus disappearing.

"Just drive fast." I murmur to Nefertiti. "But not so fast that we attract attention." I amend.

Nefertiti surprises me by doing exactly that. Dingus sits on the floor behind her shoulder giving turn-by-turn directions. We stay north on I-5 for a long time before taking an exit that leads deep into the mountains. When there's wide open space and no other cars around, she doesn't hesitate to press the gas pedal all the way down.

Free of pursuit, Nefertiti and I take turns driving east all night and half the next day. We roll across the state line into Illinois on Sunday afternoon.

And the engine dies — again.

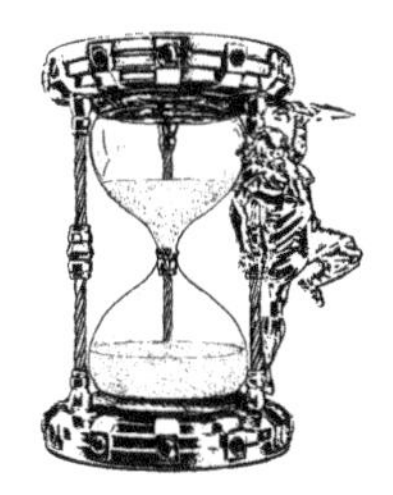

He only vomits when he wants to

I kick the rear tire when Dingus tells me the transport is done. If he can't fix it, literally no one in this time can. The engine just isn't built for the action it has seen. We're so close and yet, so far away. We will have to walk.

Every step I take forward feels like another wasted moment – one I thought we had gained with each mile in Jenny's transport. Now all that gain is washed away.

I hold on to the belief that Benny and the native are still locked up in the same place. What if Pheloni moved them? There's no reason to hold either of them in a hospital once the native's wounds heal. They have no reason to hold Benny at all.

But I remember what Pheloni said that day when we were hiding in the dumpster. *You'll be back.* He's holding them as bait. That means they must still be in the same place. Otherwise Pheloni would give us some kind of hint as to a new location.

I'm starving and my feet hurt so bad I want them to fall off for relief. But my adrenaline keeps me moving. Soon, the sun dips toward the horizon indicating evening. We make it to a fueling station. While Nefertiti and Jamie find a sanitation room, Dingus and I study half of a modular house perched on the back of a flat trailer. Just beyond that truck is another, carrying what could only be the other half of the same house. Two small cars are parked between the trucks. One has an *Oversized Load* sign on it and the other has a *Windy City* bumper sticker. Chicago is the Windy City! It's a good sign.

I run my hand along the heavy plastic that encloses and protects the house where the two halves will eventually fit together. The sheets of plastic are attached to a wood frame with heavy-duty staples. I am trying to work one of the staples loose with my fingernail when someone suddenly appears on the other side of the plastic. "Geez, Dingus! How'd you get in there?"

"Through the door." Dingus points to the end of the trailer. "It wasn't locked."

"Stay there. I'll get Nefertiti and Jamie." I run back across the parking lot and see they are just coming out of the building. "C'mon. We found the perfect truck."

Nefertiti grabs Jamie's hand and holds him in place. "I'm not sure I want to do this. It's dangerous. Besides, we could end up in Texas."

"This whole trip is dangerous. And this truck is going to Chicago, I'm sure of it."

"How do you know?"

"It just has to." I point to the bumper sticker, knowing it is no guarantee but I can't accept any other thought. We are on the north side of the highway and the truck is facing north. If the truck takes an exit, we can get off and find another truck. "Trust me," I say.

A group of men bustle past us toward the trucks. "C'mon Nefertiti. We'll never make it on foot."

When I see the same group of men standing in front of one of the trucks, I leave knowing Nefertiti will follow. She's as exhausted as I am. The men separate and each gets into one of the trucks or cars. I look back to Nefertiti. "Hurry! They're going to leave without us. Dingus is already in the truck!"

"Oh!" Nefertiti tugs Jamie's hand and runs along with me. We sneak up behind one of the trucks and climb in through the door that Dingus holds open. As I shut the door behind me, the engine rumbles and, after a minute, the whole house vibrates and rocks so hard, that we all fall to the floor.

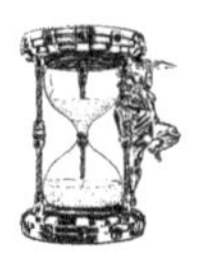

We ride a very long time and are able to get a little sleep. I wake up after about an hour and Dingus is sitting on the floor holding his stomach. It's dark, but a passing streetlight illuminates Dingus' face through the plastic. He looks green.

On the bright side, we're moving. And each mile brings us closer to Chicago. I peek through the plastic and watch the road signs to make sure we are still on Route 55. Jamie plays a Viarbox game in the expanse of the empty living room. Nefertiti and I practice flinging marbles. It's impossible to hit any targets in a dark moving vehicle, but I'm getting good at flicking the marble with some power. I offer to let Dingus have a turn, but he just groans.

"Do you want me to turn you off?" I ask.

Dingus holds his stomach and shakes his head.

"It's your funeral… er… I mean. Say the word if you change your mind. Once we get home, you'll feel a lot better, okay?"

"Is he doing this on purpose?" Nefertiti asks.

I shake my head. "Not this time."

It's hard to see in the dark, but I can tell when we turn off the highway and onto a smaller road. I hope they stop soon. I saw a highway sign for Chicago, but I didn't catch how many miles it said.

When the truck finally stops and the engine shuts down, Nefertiti and I drag Dingus to join us in a closet in case the men come inside. Instead, I hear the smaller transport doors close and drive away. Three of us step down out of the house. Jamie rubs his many bruises gained by playing Viarbox in a moving arena.

"Two-thirty," I mumble, looking at my watch.

Dingus finally steps out of the house. He actually looks better. His face is no longer green. But, there's some sort of gray slime on his shirt.

"Woof! You okay?" I ask, waiving my hand in front of my nose.

"Yeah." Dingus sounds better, too.

"You smell like barf!"

"You should smell the house." Dingus grins.

Nefertiti is now greener than Dingus.

When he looks down to study the barf on his shirt, Dingus' eyes narrow. "What's this?" He picks a small piece of technology out of the slime on his belly. Finding a clean spot near the hem of his shirt, he wipes it and holds it up to his face for closer inspection. His eyes widen.

"What is it?" I ask.

Dingus puts a finger to his mouth to shush me. Then he yawns loudly. "We should rest here and find our way to Chicago in the morning." When I start to protest, Dingus puts his hand over my mouth and whispers, "Say 'Okay'."

"Uh… Okay," I say when he removes his hand.

"Over there is a good place," Jamie says, pointing to a field.

"Yes, that looks like a great place." Dingus says, enunciating every word carefully. "Come on."

Then he drops the device to the ground and steps on it with the toe of his sneaker. He grinds it into the dirt again and again. When he removes his foot, the device is a mangled mess of microscopic nothing. "I really did have a bug," Dingus explains, still looking at the object.

"I thought you couldn't get human diseases," Nefertiti says.

Dingus shakes his head. "Not that kind of bug. A listening device. The kind a spy uses."

"But how…" I don't have to finish my question because the answer is obvious. "Pheloni! When he grabbed you in Philadelphia." I smack my forehead. "Oh man, that's how he kept finding us. Which means he knows we're here. He's probably already setting a trap for us."

Dingus fingers the barf on his shirt. "You can refresh me now."

"Ha! You wish!" But, I get out my pocket pilot and click it twice.

Dingus reappears and his stomach gives a loud rumble. He reaches in his pocket and gets out a pack of crackers from his stash.

I smile. I am so relieved to have my best friend back. It wasn't the time travel after all. Maybe I can keep Dingus with me in 1976. If Dingus will stay.

"We should get going," I say. "I hope we're close enough to Chicago. This doesn't look like a big city to me." But in the distance, the big city lights echo off the overcast sky like a beacon calling us home.

We walk without making camp. I can't see well enough to find a decent place to sleep and we're too close to want to.

Sometime after three o'clock in the morning Nefertiti finds a booth for an old-fashioned conferencer. A big book with names and numbers in it hangs from a chain and Nefertiti flips through it before contacting for a public transport.

It takes the last dime of Benny's virtual money to pay for the ride to the hospital. We fall slightly short of cash and the crabby driver speeds off making an obscene gesture out the window. He'll be even crabbier when the virtual money disappears after he gets out of range from Dingus.

Now we just need to wait until the hospital opens to people who don't have blood gushing out of them. We rest across the highway at the train station.

I sit with my back against the wall, satisfied.

Dingus leans back next to me and puts his hands behind his head. "I'd say that was pretty uneventful."

Nefertiti picks up and throws a small stone at him. "Are you kidding? That was completely eventful."

Dingus shrugs. "We're here, aren't we?" His belly gives a loud rumble in protest.

I slap him on the shoulder. "Glad to have you back, Buddy."

Nefertiti rolls her eyes and yawns. "Veebs," she mumbles.

I watch as Nefertiti's and Jamie's eyelids heavily lay down to rest. Their breathing turns light and steady and I know they're asleep. I should do the same but my mind is still active. I glance at Dingus. He narrows his eyes. "You're going home right?" he whispers.

I don't answer. I won't lie, but not answering is as good as telling Dingus the truth, that I am going to stay in 1976.

"Then I'm staying with you," Dingus says.

I feel better about staying now that Dingus will be with me. We don't need to discuss it any more.

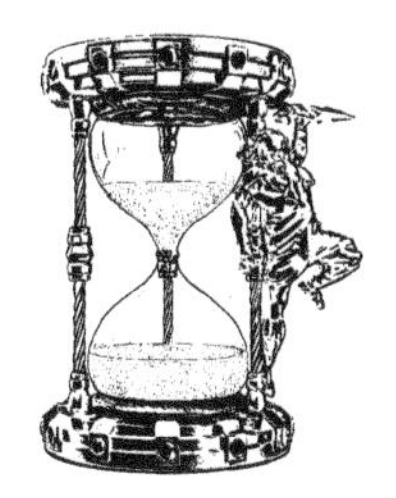

Playing with fire and blowing things up

I don't remember dozing, but I must have. When I open my eyes, it is light. I've grown used to waking in strange places and spare no time sorting out the morning confusion. It's Monday morning. We have only two days left.

People are staring at us so I nudge Dingus. He looks like he's just coming out of sleep mode. "Er… Mom will be here any minute." I open my eyes wide, practically stretching my eyebrows up to my hairline. Then I flick my head to the side. "We should go over there and watch for her."

Dingus looks around at the people. "Oh! Yes. Mom. Let's go." Dingus gives Jamie and Nefertiti each a tap on the foot. We all get up and walk down the stairs and over the bridge to the hospital.

We follow a few adults into the hospital, managing to avoid suspicious glares. Once inside, we follow the path that Pheloni took us a week ago. We need to know if Benny and the native are still here.

If they are, Pheloni will be expecting us. But if we hurry, he might not expect us so early. Hopefully, he thinks we're just waking up in a field far away.

It will be tricky. We need to search the corridors, but can't risk confrontation. Nefertiti finds a laundry closet that we use as our headquarters. She and Jamie wait there while Dingus and I peer around the corner into the lounge area where we waited for Benny a week earlier. The woman is at her post. I'm sure the door is locked. We have to get buzzed in. But how?

Dingus pulls my sleeve and whispers. "Click me to the other side of the door. I'll open the door from the inside if the coast is clear. If I don't open the door in five seconds, click me back and run back to the closet. That will mean someone saw me."

The scheme works. When I see the door open, I crouch down and duck-walk under the receptionist's window to the door. Once inside, I face a long corridor of rooms. A chair sits in front of one of the rooms, but otherwise the corridor is empty. On the other hand, there's nowhere to hide if someone comes in. So we have to be quick. Each door has a window. I send Dingus down one side of the hallway, while I take the other.

I peer through each window as I make my way up the hall. When the patient inside isn't Benny or the native, I move on to the next. When I get to the room with the empty chair outside the door, I look in the window.

Jackpot! I waive Dingus over to me.

Benny is wearing green hospital pajamas and reclining on his bed like a normal patient. He looks healthy – not tortured or haggard in any way.

Then I see him. The native. My breath catches in excitement, as if I'm seeing a fairy tale character. The last time I saw the native was in the bronze bowl. Like Jamie and Father Serra, he's like a Viarbox character come to life. The native is wearing green pajama pants, but his chest is bare. Instead of bloodied, his shoulder is wrapped in a white bandage. He sits cross legged on the second bed. Benny talks to him and the native chuckles as if Benny said something funny.

I try to open the door. Of course it's locked. I tap on the window.

Benny leaps off the bed toward the door. I put my finger to my mouth and wink.

Benny almost laughs. He winks back. Then he gets a curious look on his face and the direction of his gaze flicks down to the empty chair and back up to me.

"Where's the guard?" he calls through the window.

My eyes widen. *Guard?*

I shake my head to Benny. I don't want to shout and risk being heard. I don't know where the guard is.

"He's usually there," Benny says. "He might have just gone to the bathroom. You'd better get out of here."

Dingus bends down and studies the lock on the door.

"Can you unlock it?" I whisper.

Dingus straightens up and reaches into his pocket. "Yeah, I have a tool…," he stops talking when I hear a man's voice coming from the opposite end of the hall.

"Click me into the room, quick!" Dingus says. "Then go back to the laundry closet and wait five minutes before clicking me back. I'll find out what I can and we'll make a plan from there."

The owner of the voice hasn't yet turned the corner. So I do as Dingus said. I click him into the room while I'm heading down the hall. I quietly open the outer door and duck walk back past the receptionist and run all the way back to our closet.

Nefertiti is oddly dressed and rummaging through bins of fabric. She straightens and looks nervous when I enter. But, her face relaxes when she sees it's just me. "Is everything okay? Where's Dingus?"

"Yeah, we found them. I put Dingus in the room with them to find out what he can. What are you doing?" I touch the white smock she's wearing.

"A disguise. If someone sees us, maybe I can pretend to be a doctor. We were just looking for a gown to make Jamie look like a patient when you came in. You're not just gonna leave Dingus in there are you?"

"No. I'll bring him back in a couple minutes. He's finding out as much as he can. There's a guard stationed by his room. Maybe Benny will have figured out a schedule."

"Did ye see the a-gent?" Jamie asks.

"No, he wasn't there."

"Let's finish our disguises. We might need them." Nefertiti turns back to her rummaging. She's tall enough to maybe pull it off – if no one looks at her face directly. Do surgeons wear their masks outside the operating room? Jamie and I could never get away with looking like anything more than pediatric patients. That wouldn't give us cause to be up on the secure ward. There were no children in any of the rooms that I saw.

When sufficient time has gone by, I click to bring Dingus back to our laundry hideout. The small room is already cramped before Dingus' arrival. He puts us over the edge and Jamie has to climb inside a laundry cart to make room.

"What did he say?" I ask.

"Well," Dingus blushes. "He's not happy about us wrecking his plane."

With everything that happened this past week, I had forgotten all about that. I give Dingus a gesture that says, "And…" and wait for him to get to the important part.

"And…" Dingus continues, "I told him we're going to get him out. There's a guard posted all the time, except when he uses the sanitation room. We just picked a lucky moment. But, the night guard flirts with the nurses and is often away from his post."

"Good," I say.

"He also says their meals are very specific. The kitchen makes up every tray special and writes the intended room and bed number on a piece of paper. We can slip a note with instructions to him if we can find his tray. His room number is A723, and his bed number is one. Two Feathers' bed number is two."

"Two Feathers?"

"That's the native's name. Two Feathers."

"Two Feathers," Jamie tries the name out.

"Does he speak English?" I ask. "I saw Benny talking to him in the window."

"He understands simple stuff," Dingus explains. "Especially when you talk with your hands. Benny's been doing a lot of charades to help him learn. Luckily, he's from the Potawatomi tribe and my translator knows that language. He was a little weirded out by the speaker, but… I guess everything is weird to him right now, so it wasn't that bad. He seemed glad to be able to speak in his own language, so I left the translators with him and Benny. Benny can explain everything to him a little better now."

"Okay," I say. We have two full days left. I want to start making a plan. "So we know how to get a message to him if we have to. And we know that sometimes the guard slips away at night. We also know his door is locked." I look at Dingus. "Were you able to try the lock while you were there?"

"No," Dingus says. "But I caught a look at it and I'm not worried."

I smile. He's probably right. These primitive locks will be no match for Dingus. "What about the agent? Did Benny mention him?"

Dingus nods. "He says Pheloni hasn't been around all week. He interrogated both Benny and Two Feathers early on and must have realized neither of them knew anything. They've just been locked up ever since. Other than meals, an occasional cleaning woman, and a nurse who checks Two Feathers' bandage once a day, no one bothers them. Even the guard just sits outside the door. He doesn't talk to them. I told him about our troubles with Pheloni. That would explain why he hadn't seen him much."

"He's using them as bait," I say with certainty. "He's here."

"And waiting for us," Nefertiti says.

"Yes," I agree. "I wish Benny could communicate with us better in case Pheloni..."

"He can!" Nefertiti interrupts me. She digs in her pocket and pulls out her conference. "We can write him a note to explain how to use this and slip it into his meal tray. Then he can communicate with us any time."

"Good thinking," I say. "Except there's a lot people in the cafeteria. I think the kitchen would notice if a bunch of kids started snooping around."

Then I notice Jamie sitting in the laundry cart. He's small enough to fit. I snap my fingers. "You can dress up like a cleaning person, Nefertiti, and take Jamie in the cart. Wait until mealtime. Then, when the food cart comes to his floor, you roll the cleaning cart up the hall, park next to the food cart while the meal delivery person is in one of the rooms. Then stand guard while Jamie slips the conferencer onto Benny's tray." I turn to Jamie before continuing. "Hide it under a napkin or something so it's out of sight."

Jamie smiles, looking happy to have a role.

"Can you read, Jamie?"

"A wee bit. I know letters and numbers."

Dingus reaches into his pocket and pulls out a pen. "Give me your arm," he says to Jamie. When Jamie presents his arm, Dingus writes the room number on it. "You have to look for that number. There might be a slip of paper or something that tells the meal delivery people which trays go to which room."

Jamie nods. "I will do it."

"You have to be very quick," I say. "And you can't let anyone see you. Remember, the meal people won't be in the rooms for long. The room doors are clustered in fours down the hall, so you'll only have as long as it takes to deliver eight meals to four rooms. But the person will be in and out of the rooms to come for the next tray, so you must listen and stay hidden. Be very careful." I lift my head to Nefertiti. "Try to catch the food tray when it's as far away from the guard as possible so he doesn't notice any movement."

"Right," Nefertiti says.

We are too late to catch the breakfast trays, so we test Nefertiti's disguise on a lower floor while we wait. I hear a nurse mention that lunch would arrive at eleven thirty.

We go back to our laundry hideout to wait. When the time comes, I have to pace in the tiny linen closet alone. I have no role in this expedition and the wait is excruciating. Nefertiti took Dingus along with her in the form of my pocket pilot. If the guard is not at his post, she can click Dingus in to unlock the door right then and there. If the guard is there, then they will stick with Plan A.

My heart leaps when the door opens. I breathe out in relief when Nefertiti rolls the cart back in with Jamie. Her smile tells me the mission is a success.

"I did it!" Jamie jumps out of the cart like a Jack-in-the-Box.

"He was perfect!" Nefertiti beams. I hold out my hand and Nefertiti hands over the pocket pilot. I click Dingus on and share the good news.

It takes only a few seconds for my pocket pilot to buzz. I click to answer. "Benny?"

Yeah, it's me. Holy cow, I can see your head! I hear a crash as Benny drops the conference. After he gets it back in his hands, he continues. *You got mashed potatoes on your phone.*

"It won't hurt it. We're going to get you out, but we need a plan. We can unlock your door, but we have to wait for the guard to leave. From what Dingus said, it sounds like night time is the best time."

Yeah. The night guard is often up wandering around. Oh, by the way… Benny's voice switches to a loud whisper. *What the heck did you do to my plane?*

"Why did you rat us out?" I throw back at him.

I didn't think he'd believe me. This guy's intent on finding you kids. He wants your time travel program.

"Yeah, we kind of figured that out. He's not real nice about it either."

Benny whispers… *Gotta go. Someone's coming.*

"What happened?" I ask when Benny calls back.

Pheloni's back! Good grief, that's the first I've seen him all week. That was too close. Do you think he knows you're here? I mean, it's weird that you show up and then he's just a minute behind you. I'm in the bathroom in case he comes back.

Dingus reaches over and takes my pocket pilot. He whispers into it. "Benny, whisper. Can you hear me? Pheloni might have planted a bug. He did the same to us. Be careful what you say. Check all your pockets. Change your clothes if you have something different."

The hairs on the back of my neck stand at attention. That was suspiciously close. Pheloni must know we're here. I whisper, "Benny, we've got to work out a plan, so we're going to sign off. Just get in touch with us if you have to. We'll do the same. But be careful.

Roger

"Roger?"

Roger. I mean, right. Yes. Now go!

I click off the pocket pilot. It's time to make a plan. "I think we're going to need a diversion," I say.

Dingus smiles at that. It's the kind of smile that always gets me into trouble. This time, I'm glad for it. I waggle my eyebrows and smile back at Dingus.

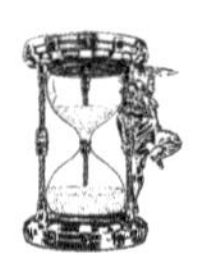

The four of us walk nearly a mile to find the perfect neighborhood for our mission. I know it's wrong, but this is an emergency and we can't come back empty handed. Nefertiti, Jamie and I wait a block away for Dingus to get the items we needed.

He took the empty backpack with him; the former contents of which are well-hidden in our closet at the hospital. I keep one eye on the time and the other over my shoulder. After what seems like forever, I finally see Dingus sprinting up the alley.

"Go, go, go!" he says in a loud whisper. "Move!"

"Did you get it?" I say over my shoulder as I run.

"Yeah," he says. "Shut up and run!" The backpack is practically bursting at the seams.

I run, checking now and then to make sure everyone is keeping up. We run for three blocks when Dingus finally slows. "I… can't…"

Dingus doesn't have the stamina to keep going. I look back in the direction we came from. "I don't think anyone's coming."

Dingus looks back. "No," he says, breathing hard. "I didn't… see anyone."

"Geez, Dingus. What'd you get us all excited for if no one's coming?"

"You… never know."

Nefertiti groans and gives Dingus a look, but keeps her mouth shut. Jamie is dancing around like he wants to run some more.

"So how'd you make out?" I say to Dingus.

"Piece… of cake." He says, still breathing heavy. He pulls the backpack off his shoulder and opens it, revealing two car stereo speakers and some wire that he swiped from an unlocked transport.

"Well, that's it." Nefertiti throws her arms out. "We're officially thieves."

"It's for a good cause," Dingus assures us.

"This idea of yours better be a good one," I say.

Dingus gives his eyebrows a dance. "Trust me!"

"Now Dingus," Nefertiti says in a motherly voice. "No playing with fire and blowing things up, okay?"

"Aww, you take all the fun out of a covert operation!"

We spend some time assembling Dingus' big idea. Then when there's nothing left to do, we try to rest as best as we can while we wait. Jamie curls up in the laundry cart. Dingus leans against the cart on guard duty. Nefertiti and I are on a pile of blankets and clothes on the floor. Even though it's cramped, I had so little sleep these past few days that it's not hard to doze off.

Dingus wakes us up a little past midnight. "It's time."

The good news about being so late at night is there are few people around to notice us. The bad news is that the empty corridors make us stand out like Rex on a suburban sidewalk.

We each carry a part of the rescue operation: the speakers, wires, a crude wooden box and the Viarbox earpiece. Dingus has the backpack, which once again holds the toys. We move swiftly down the hall. The receptionist is gone. There is no one in the darkened waiting area.

I peer through the window. The hallway is quiet. The guard is not off flirting with nurses around the corner, as I hoped. He's asleep in his chair. It's okay, though. We planned for this.

"He's asleep." I whisper to the others. "Is everyone ready?"

No one answers.

"Good! Let's go."

Dingus pulls a small tool out of his pocket and easily unlocks the door.

I creep through the open doorway. I can hear the guard snoring all the way down the hall. I have the two speakers connected to each other with a wire, which also connects to the small, crudely made box that Jamie carries. A short electrical cord is connected to the box. Another wire connects my speakers to the Viarbox earpiece, which Nefertiti has.

Once through the door, we take up our predetermined positions. Jamie stays by the door and sets the box down in the corner. I watch as he plugs in the cord and I nod confirmation that he did it correctly. He beams at me, enjoying being part of the operation.

I place the speakers along the wall halfway down the hall. Dingus helps Nefertiti unroll the remaining wire as they creep quietly toward the sleeping guard. Nefertiti takes her position behind the guard with the earpiece ready to go.

Dingus gently sets the backpack on the floor and goes to work unlocking the door to room number 723. He fumbles and drops the tool, which clanks to the floor. The sleeping guard twitches and snorts. Dingus gives an apologetic look to Nefertiti. She looks like she's ready to grab the backpack and whack him with it. I am by Dingus' side, poised and ready to run into the room. I motion for Dingus to hurry up.

The door to Room 723 clicks open.

"Hold it right there!" The guard's voice breaks the silence.

Nefertiti slaps the earpiece on his head and flicks the visual button. The guard screams in terror and waives his arms in front of him. He falls to the floor. Two nurses appear at the end of the hall.

I waive my arms at Jamie, who pushes the button on the speakers. The roar of the virtual Rex, which the guard is now seeing, rings through the hall along with a virtual explosion.

The nurses scream and run into each other. They turn and run back around the corner. More screams come from behind nearby doors. I dash into Room 723. Two Feathers is squatting on the bed prepared for a fight.

"Not real!" I shout. "No animal. Come with me." We had explained our plan to them earlier over the conference, but I imagine Rex is a scary sound to anyone.

Benny is on his feet and beside me. I lead him and Two Feathers out of the room and send them toward the rear exit along with Nefertiti, Dingus and Jamie. They run past the guard, who is now in a fetal position on the floor. I watch until all five are through the Exit door.

I pull the earpiece from the paralyzed guard. As I am about to run to join the others, two arms gather around my middle and lift me off the floor. I smell the garlic before I hear the voice.

"Got you!" Agent Pheloni shoves me into Room 723 and yanks the pocket pilot from my shorts as I fall away from him. He slams the door. I jump and pound my fist into the other side of it. "Noooo!"

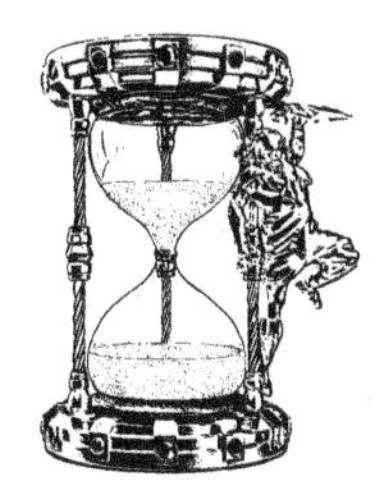

A reluctant lesson in time travel

The corridor outside Room 723 is crawling with police and security in a matter of minutes. I lean against the door listening to the sounds from the hall. Someone finally unplugs the box at the end of the hall and the Rex noises are silenced.

"Put that down. It's evidence."

I jump up to look out the window. Pheloni yanks the backpack out of one of the security officer's hands.

"Dinguuuus!" I yell to the ceiling. "You yoctobrain!" I reach for my pocket pilot, but it's not there.

"That's not evidence," I yell through the door. "It's mine!"

Pheloni presses his forehead to the window and looks down his nose at me. "It *was* yours," he says with a sneer.

I kick the door, wishing it was Pheloni's shin. Then I turn my back and slide to the floor to wait for the commotion to quiet down in the hall. Eventually it does. Next time I peek out the window, the hall is empty. I hope the others got away. We really botched this. I should have switched roles with Dingus and left him behind. Then I could click him back like in Philadelphia. At least I'm sure he's already working on a plan to rescue me.

I sit on the bed closest to the door and don't have to wait long before I hear the key in the lock. Before I know what's happening, Pheloni tosses the backpack on the bed, tackles me, flips me on my belly, and handcuffs me. Then he lifts me by the shirt and places me on the bed closest to the window. The backpack remains on the opposite bed.

I watch helplessly as Pheloni dumps the contents of the pack onto the other bed. He methodically sorts the objects into what appears to be toys in one pile and tools in another. In the middle, Pheloni places objects that I assume he can't tell whether it's a toy or a tool. My pocket pilot is in the middle pile.

"Now then," Pheloni says with a calm voice. "Let's take a look at what you thought was so important to bring with you from the future, shall we?"

"Don't bother. It's just dumb toys," I say.

Undaunted, Pheloni holds up the toy transports. "Tell me about these."

What is there to say? They're just transports. It's obvious. I say as much to Pheloni.

"Do they run on a track?"

Pheloni seems genuinely interested, so I elaborate. "Yeah. You can buy kits with tracks. They hover above them and race around like normal. You can get race tracks, city tracks, country roads. You can build a whole network of roads and places for them to go."

"That must be a lot of fun for kids… in your time."

I meet Pheloni's eyes. He's looking for confirmation. I give a noncommittal answer. "I'm too old for that, now. These were from when I was younger."

"Then, why do you carry them with you?"

I shrug. "I just grabbed the pack without thinking what was in it." That's actually the truth.

He nods. "What do you play now that you're older?"

I point my chin at the Viarbox gear. "Virtual reality games."

Pheloni picks up the earpiece and asks me to explain. I do. Pheloni is patient through my explanation, asking questions and encouraging me to talk about an average day in my time.

He holds up the roll of tape. "Anything special about this?"

"I don't think so. It's just a roll of tape."

Satisfied, Pheloni moves it aside and holds up a container of pills. He shakes it and looks up at me. "Vitamins?"

"Nanobot pills. These change your hair color. Um... I got them last Halloween. But you can get all kinds. Change your eye color, paint your nails, polka dot your skin... You need a prescription to cure a disease or get a nose job or something like that."

He smiles and puts them down. He moves on to the mangowand. "This?"

"It reverses magnetism," I say.

"And why would you want to do that?"

"It can fix things." I lift a shoulder and let it fall. "Or mess them up if you want."

He scans the assortment and shakes his head. "Which one is the time travel device?"

Ah, now we're getting to it. To stall, I reposition myself on the bed. The man's eyes stay trained on me.

"None of them," I say. "It's not here."

Pheloni's smile fades, replaced by a blank look. His thin lips press together, making them nearly disappear. He takes a deep breath and lets it out before his smile returns.

"Surely, you must have the device with you. How else will you get home?" He looks expectantly at me.

I don't want to answer that line of questions. Pheloni must have sensed it because he picks up another item that seems like a safe topic. I explain the perpetual flashlight and Pheloni is satisfied with my explanation.

When he picks up the pocket pilot, I lunge toward it. I feel helpless and naked without it, like Dingus must feel when his arm disappears. I struggle against the handcuffs, itching to reach for it but my hands are secure behind me.

Pheloni pushes me back onto the bed. "Oh, this must be important." For a split second, I see the sneer before it switches back to a smile. "Tell me about it."

I have to tell the man *something*. Maybe only part of the truth. "It's my pocket pilot." That is the truth. "It does a lot of things, but mostly it's a communicator."

"That's it? It's a telephone?"

"Yes. It does other things too, but just normal stuff."

Pheloni's mouth turns up even higher. He seems delighted with my answer. "Just normal stuff, you say?" I nod. Pheloni continues. "Normal stuff like… time travel?"

I shake my head. "No. I told you, the time travel device isn't here."

"Then why did you flinch when I touched it?" Pheloni's smile and eyes remain kind, but his voice rises to a higher pitch, sending me a hint of danger.

"I keep it with me all the time. I feel strange without it attached to my belt. I'm just glad to see it."

"I'm sure you are." Now Pheloni's voice is soft, almost a whisper. "And you're going to tell me about every single thing this pocket pilot does. Just like you told me about the toys and other… stuff." Pheloni opens his jacket, revealing his gun and a very large knife.

I begin to sweat. The man is just trying to intimidate me. It's working. I need to stall. *Think, think, think!* If I tell Pheloni the pocket pilot really is the time travel program, maybe he will let me go.

"Okay, okay! I'll tell you whatever you want to know!"

He closes his jacket and smiles. "Good choice."

"Yes! That's it."

He raises both eyebrows. "What's it?"

"The pocket pilot. It's how we got here. It's the time travel device."

"How does it work?"

"You have to press the buttons in the right sequence."

Pheloni leans in and unleashes a load of garlic breath at close range. "Tell me the sequence and remember that no one knows you exist in this time. *No one* will miss you."

"But, but... You're an FBI agent. You're supposed to protect people."

"I'll be an FBI agent with a time machine." Pheloni shoves the pocket pilot under my nose. "Now, tell me how it works."

"It... It..." I try to keep my brain from melting. How can I make this work to my advantage? The pocket pilot can't harm Pheloni.

"Tell me the correct sequence to activate the time portal."

Portal? There's no portal. I spew out a random list of colored buttons. I know nothing will happen but Pheloni follows my instructions.

"Nothing's happening." He looks up and doesn't look happy.

"One more," I say. "T... turn the pilot around b... backwards and click the big blue button in the corner. The portal will open up in front of you."

Pheloni does it. "Where's the portal?"

"It's invisible. It's right in front of you. But don't step in it just yet. Not until you know where you're going."

"How do you find out? Is there a way to steer this thing?" Pheloni looks up at me with a mixture of excitement, greed, and sincere curiosity on his face. A millisecond later, his eyes bulge when a bedside lamp slams into the back of his head. He falls to the floor between the two beds.

Dingus stands behind him like an avenging angel.

"Thanks, buddy," I say without surprise. I had given Pheloni the special sequence to power off Dingus from a distance rather than the single refresher click. The big blue button turned Dingus back on inside the room. Putting the pilot backward placed him behind Pheloni instead of in front of him. Luckily, Dingus was quick to analyze the situation.

"Get me out of these." I turn my back to let Dingus work on the handcuffs.

He has them off in a nanosecond. While Dingus goes to work on the door lock, I gather the toys into the backpack. On the way out, I hook the pocket pilot onto my shorts, feeling whole again. Dingus locks the room with an unconscious Pheloni still inside.

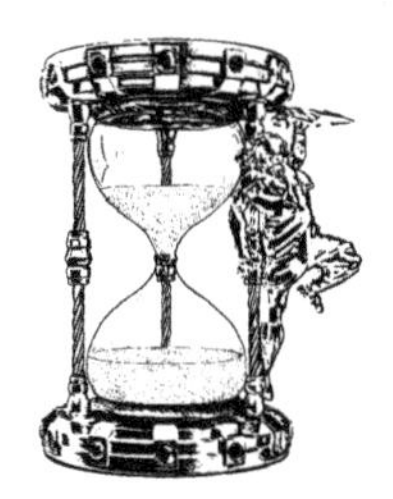

Both feet in the game

Twenty minutes later, Dingus and I join the others in the hotel room that Benny had arranged and paid for. It's nicer and cleaner than the previous one and it has two double beds instead of one small rickety bed. The only similarity is that everyone is eating pizza.

Nefertiti is sitting on the floor but she jumps up when she sees me. But, instead of hugging me, she hugs Dingus. "I knew as soon as you disappeared, you'd get him back. Thank you."

Dingus' face turns bright red. I can swear the corners of his mouth turn up for just a split second. Then Nefertiti hugs me. "I'm glad you're back."

Everyone else pats me on the back as I work my way through the room. With six people in the room, there's nowhere to sit but on the floor.

"Oh my goodness!" Benny says. "What have I gotten myself into?"

"I'm really sorry about the trouble," I say. "And your transport… er, airplane. Dingus didn't mean to crash it."

"Well, at least it's insured," Benny says, waving the thought away. "But, I'm probably on the FBI's most wanted list now."

"I don't think so," I say. "Pheloni seems to be working outside of his job responsibilities. He just wants the time travel program." I explain what happened to me after they left the hospital.

"We can stay and try to help you if I'm wrong," I offer to Benny. He lifts a shoulder and lets it drop. "I'm a big boy. But, what about you guys and Two Feathers? And what's up with the new kid?" He gestures toward Jamie.

"Two Feathers," I say, finally having the opportunity to meet the native.

"Two Feathers," he repeats back to me.

"He speaks English?" I ask.

Benny shrugs. "You spend a week locked in a room with someone and you'll pick up their language in a hurry. Dingus' translator helped too. What's up with the new kid?" He repeats. "Is this the one from Philadelphia? Why'd you bring him here?"

"He's an orphan," Nefertiti says.

"He has no home. So we're taking him with us," I add.

"He's not a puppy, Nikola," Benny warns. "You can't just keep him. People will want to know where he came from. They'll want to see his birth certificate. He needs a Social Security number. People need to have records and he doesn't have any."

"Okay!" I say. "I get it." I look up at Nefertiti. "We'll think of something."

Nefertiti goes over to Two Feathers and touches the bandage on his shoulder. "What's going to happen to you when you go back? I mean back to your own time?" she says.

"What going happen?" Two Feathers repeats.

"You were wounded when you were displaced," she says. "We saw it. You were fighting a battle and you were shot. If we send you back, you'll return to the same place, the same moment you left."

"Two Feathers brave warrior. Go back."

"Yes, but you were fighting," Nefertiti says.

"Fighting," Two Feathers says, nodding. "Gun." He points to his wound and then opens his arms. "Land change. Two Feathers dead. Come here."

I nearly choked on my pizza. "Does he think he's dead?" I ask Benny.

"No. We talked about that."

"Does he understand we mean to send him back?"

Two Feathers answers for himself, "Go back. Not dead. Yes."

I turn to Two Feathers. "Do you understand you're going back to the same moment when you left? Where the soldier was about to stab you with a knife?"

Two Feathers takes a bite of pizza. "Mm hmm."

"Are you afraid?" Nefertiti asks.

"Two Feathers brave," he says with his mouth full. He swallows the pizza and wipes his mouth with the sleeve of his hospital pajama. "Go home. Not die here."

Two Feather's declaration stuns me. He is the one person who really does have a reason to not want to go home. He was just inches from death! I saw it with my own eyes. And still, he wants to go home?

I feel the cold shiver of shame rush up my back. Here I am planning to stay in 1976 to avoid facing Daemon in the Viarbox tournament. I understand Jamie's reason for not wanting to go home. He'll be just as homeless no matter what. But going back to 1776 Philadelphia will be a harder life than he might have here or in the future.

Father Serra can live an easier life too, if he stays. But he has churches to build and California to establish.

But, Two Feathers... Instead of choosing the safety of staying put, Two Feathers is jumping in with both feet toward a very real danger. Not in a virtual world. Not in his over-zealous imagination! But for real.

What is the worst that can happen if I go back? Sucking food through a straw is just an exaggeration that my own brain invented. Sure Daemon is big, but… a steaming mass of seventh grade pulp? Pah!

He's just trying to psyche you out, Nefertiti had said. And I didn't believe her.

What was it that Father Serra told me? I should attack my enemy with friendship. I don't think that will work for Two Feathers. As for me, I don't have a whole lot of experience making friends. Although this past week might prove differently. I never knew so many people to be nice to me all at one time. Is that what they are? Friends? Human friends who aren't nice just because they were programmed that way? Nefertiti, Benny, Jamie, Jenny, Amy – even Father Serra and Pastor Bob at the mission. They were all nice to me. They're all friends.

And I've been treating them like… game pieces. I should go home and let Daemon pound me senseless for being a yoctobrain.

"You okay," Nefertiti whispers to me.

I swipe my arm across the moisture that has collected at the corners of my eyes. "Yeah, I'm fine." I look away. Then I grab her arm. "Hey Nef. Thanks."

She smiles.

I turn to Two Feathers. "Can we give you something to take back with you? Something that might help?"

"Maybe he can pull off the old Rex trick!" Dingus says. "Ha! That was classic."

"No, Technoid. He won't have time to set it up."

"I was kidding! Geez."

"You're sending him back already fixed up," Benny says. "That will give him a chance."

"And he doesn't have to return lying on his back," Dingus says. "He can return standing up. That will freak out his attacker and give him a couple seconds of advantage."

"Maybe we can give him a weapon or something," I say.

"You need to get him back on the runway, right?" Benny asks. I nod. "You'll never get a knife past airport security."

Dingus steps into a Karate stance. "Maybe we can teach him some self-defense moves."

I laugh, but have to agree. "Yeah. That's a good plan."

Two Feathers was listening. He takes a bite of pizza and nods. "Good plan."

Benny claps his hands once, which makes me jump. "I hate to be the downer of this party, but the sun will be up very soon and tomorrow's a big day. You kids need some shut eye."

Four of us sleep two to a bed while Benny and Two Feathers stretch out on the floor with the extra pillows and blankets we had found stashed in the closet.

I blink once and that's all I remember.

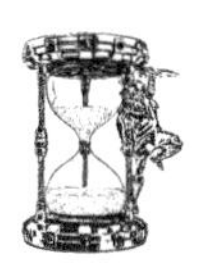

I wake up when I hear voices whispering. It must be Wednesday and a peek out the window tells me it's probably late morning. Nefertiti is leaning against the bed I'm in, writing on a piece of paper. So I slide down to the floor and sit beside her.

Benny is across the room studying Dingus at close range. "Virtual reality. When will that be invented?"

"I don't know," I say.

"Does he open up?" Benny persists. "Does he have wires and stuff?" He feels the top of Dingus' head for an opening.

"Hey!" Dingus says.

"He's not mechanical, Benny. He's virtual," I say.

"But, he's a toy, right?"

I gasp and look nervously at Dingus.

Nefertiti humphs but otherwise keeps her mouth shut.

Dingus' ears turned pink, but he doesn't explode. Instead, he patiently allows Benny to examine him.

"He's my best friend," I declare. "And he can answer for himself. You don't have to talk about him like he's not in the room."

"Oh. Sorry."

I look over Nefertiti's shoulder at her paper. "What's that?"

"I'm making a list of everything we still need to do."

"Read what you have so far," I say.

Nefertiti tucks the pencil behind her ear. "First, we have to figure out what to do with Jamie."

"I have an idea about that." Dingus pushes Benny away from his face. "I just need a computer from this time. Do they have computers in this time?"

"Businesses have computers." Benny says.

I narrow my eyes at Dingus. "What's your idea?"

Dingus waggles his eyebrows. I raise mine, but Dingus says nothing more.

I turn back to Nefertiti and nod for her to continue her list. "We have to work with Two Feathers on his re-entry," she says.

"Check." I reach out for the list and Nefertiti relinquishes it to me. I take up where she left off. "We have to get Two Feathers onto the runway." I look up at Benny. "Do you think there's more than one?"

"Ha!" Benny says. "There's definitely more than one runway."

"But how will we know which one?" I ask.

"Maybe the news reporter will remember," Nefertiti says.

"Yeah, you're right," Benny says. "I'll call the station. It'll sound better coming from an adult."

"Okay," Dingus says. "But don't say who you are for real. I can help you come up with a good lie."

"Oh Puh-leaze." Nefertiti rolls her eyes.

"Check," Benny says.

I continue from the list. "And we need to figure out how to get onto the runway once we know which one." I make a note, but no one says 'check'.

"How will you get back to your own time?" Benny asks.

"The same way as Two Feathers and Father Serra," I explain. "Dingus said the replacement sequence will work for all of us. We just have to be in the hall where you first… caught me. We'll make sure Two Feathers gets to his spot on the runway first and then we can leave him and get to our own spot."

I sit back and look over the list. "Okay, this is full of holes and we have no chance, but it's a start."

"Mr. Optimistic," Nefertiti says.

"That's why I let him hang out with me," Dingus says.

I ignore them. "The first and most important thing on the list is to figure out what to do with Jamie. Dingus, you said you had an idea."

"Oh yeah. I'll be right back," Dingus says.

"Where are you going?" Benny asks.

"Trust me!" Dingus winks at me and leaves.

"I don't like the sound of that," Benny says. "Where's he going?"

I shrug. "He can't go far; he has to stay in range. Next, we have to find out where on the runway." I look up at Benny.

Benny is at the door. "No. Seriously. What's he up to?"

"I don't know," I say. "But, he has an idea. Let him figure it out. We have our own jobs to figure out."

Benny glances once more at the door. Then he turns back to the room. He opens a few drawers in the dresser and night table until he finds a book with conferencer numbers listed in it. After flipping through the pages, he grabs Nefertiti's conferencer, studies it and hands it back to her. He holds the page up in front of her. "How do I call this number?"

Nefertiti reads the number aloud into the conferencer, clicks it once and hands it to Benny with the speaker turned on.

Someone answers at the news station. There's no visual since the other end is a conferencer from this time. Benny has a brief conversation with two separate people until he's finally transferred to the reporter who was on the scene that day.

Deidre Davenport, the voice says.

"Good morning Miss Davenport. My name is Albert..." he hesitates. "uh, Smith." He winks at me.

What can I do for you Mr. Smith?

"I think the better question is what can I do for you?"

Okay. I'll bite. What can you do for me? She sounds bored.

"Do you remember that Indian you caught on film last week?"

Yeah, I remember.

"Well," Benny takes a deep breath. "You know he escaped last night, don't you?"

Go on.

"He's with me right now," Benny says.

You're the fourth person to call about that today. How do I know he's with you and why are you volunteering to call me?

"Oh," Benny says. "I didn't count on that."

Deidre continues. *Let's get down to business, Mr. Smith. I imagine you want something in return. No one ever calls me without wanting something.*

"Just some information."

What kind of information?

"I need to know the runway number and exact location where the Indian was first spotted. Now that's not asking too much is it?"

What? I'm disappointed. No money? No reward? No fifteen-minutes-of-fame on a TV interview?

"Oh hardly. I have no desire to be seen on TV, believe me."

Why do you want to know the exact location on the runway?

"He dropped something very personal that he wants to find."

Then you're calling the wrong person. The police have already combed the runway. If he dropped something, they most likely have it as evidence.

Besides, do you honestly think you'll be allowed on the runway to look for it?

"Not really. But we'd like to know anyway."

Is that the real reason you want to know or is there something you're not telling me?

"Can you just please tell us the location?"

Okay. We were on the private runway near the back of the airport. They had to stop air traffic for an important departure.

Benny cups his hand over the conferencer's speaker. "The private runway. Of course!" Then he takes his hand away before speaking. "How far out on the runway?"

I can show the clip tonight and you can see for yourself, but I want something *in return.*

"What do you want?"

An exclusive interview with the Indian. Live. Tonight. It will tie in nicely with showing the clip again.

"No way," I say to Benny.

"You can have your interview." Benny says to Diedre. "But, it has to be over the phone."

No deal. I want him in person. It would be pointless to have him on the phone. Anyone can pretend to be him on the phone.

"We can't do that. The police will be all over us."

Deidre is quiet for a moment. *Come at 4:30 and we'll prerecord the interview and you can be long gone before it airs.*

"Deidre, you've got yourself a deal. We'll have him at the station by 4:30. And you have him out of there in plenty of time before it airs."

Excellent! Thank you, Mr. Smith.

"Thank you, Deidre."

"What did you promise in person for?" I say as soon as I hear the click of Diedre signing off.

"It'll be okay," Benny says. "We need the clip, right? Let's do what we gotta do. You'll have to take him, though."

"No, *you* take him!" Nefertiti says to Benny. "People will be happy to see you're not missing."

"Aw, I don't know," Benny says. "I'm kind of glad no one knows I'm involved in this."

"Come on, Benny," I say. "Be a hero."

"I'd rather be invisible."

"No you don't." Nefertiti picks up the backpack full of future toys and shakes it. "You want to be famous. You can't be famous if you're invisible."

"That's right!" I say. "You can use this to put yourself on the map. Tell them you weren't missing. You were simply… hibernating. You were busy researching new ideas for toys."

Benny's eyes brighten. "Yeah. I could do that." Then he looks down at his clothes, which still involve hospital pajamas. "I need to get a better suit for television," he says.

Two Feathers looks down at himself and picks up the corner of the blue hospital shirt, which hangs open, baring his chest. "Not mine," he says.

"He's right," I say. "He can't go home in that." I make a note on Nefertiti's list.

"Everything is in a locker at the hospital. I didn't think to grab them on my way out." Benny hands another number for Nefertiti to call on her conferencer. It was for the airport. After she enters it, Benny leases a small plane and schedules a flight out for tomorrow.

After his phone call, Benny and Nefertiti go shopping while Jamie, Two Feathers and I stay in the room. Jamie challenges Two Feathers to a game of marbles and we all join in. I'm actually getting good at it. We make a target and score points for hitting it. While we play, Jamie puts on the Viarbox earpiece and gloves, and is soon soaring over an early twentieth century barnyard in a Kitty Hawk Flyer.

I jump up when Dingus finally returns. He hands me two pieces of paper. After reading them, I groan. "Technoid! This is your big idea?"

"Do you have a better one?" he says.

I don't, so I fold the papers and stuff them into my pocket. "He's not going to like this."

"He'll be fine," Dingus says, dismissing the issue.

"C'mon." I tug Dingus' sleeve. "Let's practice some karate chops or something with Two Feathers."

Jamie puts his Viarbox game away and helps us move furniture to clear a space in the room. Then Dingus and I work with Two Feathers on some moves we learned in a martial arts game. Dingus pretends to be the attacking soldier. We try all different possibilities so Two Feathers can react to anything. Two Feathers gets carried away with a kick and knocks the wind out of Dingus.

"You don't have to kill the warrior," I say. "Just get him down and get away. Grab his weapon if you can. But, get back to the rest of your tribe as fast as possible. No one will ever know you were gone."

Two Feathers nods.

I hear a fumbling at the door. It's Benny and Nefertiti bringing in several large shopping bags. Jamie hops off the bed and Nefertiti dumps them onto his vacated spot.

They had found a Halloween costume shop and bought a rubber tomahawk, a quiver made of felt and cardboard with toy arrows to put in it, an Indian Chief headdress with blue feathers, and a face paint kit. Two Feathers frowns and throws the toys on the floor, but he keeps the headdress. He pulls most of the feathers out, leaving only two before placing it on his head. Then he hands one feather to each of us kids. He gathers up the rest and gives them to Benny.

An hour later, Benny and Two Feathers are ready to go. Benny wears a navy suit and tie. His shoes shine like mirrors. Two Feathers wears a brand new, genuine deerskin shirt with leather lacing at his chest and fringes down the length of his sleeves. He marvels at the elastic waistband in his deerskin pants. On his feet, he wears a pair of fringed and beaded deerskin boots that lace up nearly to his knees outside his pant legs.

Two Feathers stands next to Benny with his shoulders back and chest puffed out.

"You're looking sharp." Benny gives Two Feathers a thumbs up and clicks the side of his tongue.

"Two Feathers look sharp," he says. "Benton look sharp."

"Yeah. We're looking good." Benny squares his shoulders, mimicking Two Feathers' proud stance. "Are you ready for this?"

"Ready."

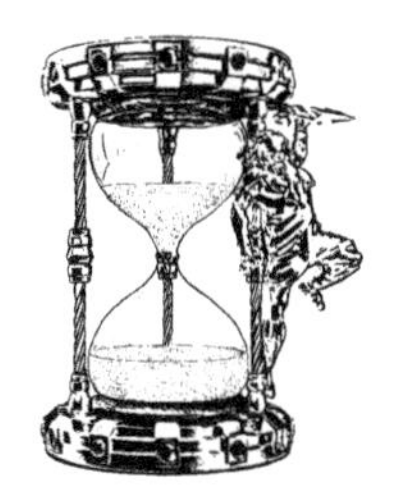

On your mark, get set, go!

This is Deidre Davenport reporting from our Chicago studio with two very special guests. If you recall, nine days ago our own news team was on location at O'Hare for the bicentennial, when we caught on film the mystifying appearance of a wounded Indian.

"Since that day, the mystery grew with a tight veil of security surrounding this young man. No one has been able to learn anything about him – who he is, where he came from, how he magically appeared on camera, or how he got onto the runway of a busy airport on the day of the bicentennial.

"The Evening News has finally caught up with him for an exclusive interview and here he is now. His name is Two Feathers." Diedre looks away from the camera and over to Two Feathers. "Hello, Two Feathers."

He leans forward to speak into the microphone. "Hello," he says. He reaches out for the microphone, but she pulls it back.

"Is Two Feathers your full name?" she asks.

"Two Feathers," he says.

"You don't look quite the same as you did last week."

Two Feathers stretches his leg out. "New shoes." He holds up his thumb and clicks the side of his tongue. "Two Feathers look sharp."

Diedre looks at his feet, "Nice." Then up to his face, "When I last saw you, you were bleeding. I understand you were shot. What can you tell me about that?"

"Two Feathers fight warrior. Shoot gun."

"Was your life in danger?"

Two Feathers touches his shoulder. "Better now."

"I'm glad you're doing well. The big question, of course, is how did you appear like magic on the runway?"

"Magic," Two Feathers says.

"Was it magic?" she asks again.

"What magic?"

"I think he doesn't understand the question," Benny says.

Deidre looks back to the camera. "Yes, in a double surprise tonight, I am also delighted to welcome Albert Bennington, the toy maker, who was reported missing since July fourth. Mr. Bennington. Welcome." The camera pans out to show both Benny and Two Feathers sitting side-by-side.

"Thank you," Benny says.

"There are so many questions; I hardly know where to begin. First, can you help answer the question about Two Feathers' appearance?"

"Yes, I'm sorry. His English is coming along well, but he's not there yet." Benny turns to Two Feathers. "How did you get here?"

Two Feathers answers. "Benton take."

"No, not right here today. I mean here from when you were home."

Two Feathers turns to Deidre. "Two Feathers fight. Warrior shoot gun. Two Feathers dead. Wake here."

"I don't understand," Deidre says.

"Maybe I can answer," Benny says. "He was being chased by some gang kids. You know how gangs call each other warriors now, right?"

"They do?"

"Sure. They shot him and almost stabbed him. In his attempt to escape, he managed to scale the fence at the airport without being seen. Until your news crew caught him on tape. The sudden appearance? Well, I hate to disappoint you, but there's no magic involved. It was a fluke. He was running and he fell."

"Mr. Bennington, how is it that you were missing and then showed up at the same time and with Two Feathers? What is your involvement?"

"Coincidence," he says. "I was never missing. I was in Europe doing research on some new toys I'm developing. The kids are going to love this new project. Keep your eye on BenCo Toys!"

He poses for the camera the same way he posed for his picture on his toy labels.

"And then what?" Deirdre asks.

Benny shrugs. "I learned my plane was stolen so I came back to the states. Turns out the thieves who stole my plane were the same thugs who attacked Two Feathers. I was questioned by the same officials, which is where I met him. Since he knows no one else, I decided to look after him for a bit. Both of us are still news mysteries, so we came here to clear it all up. It really isn't much of a mystery."

"All right. Benny!" I shout to the TV while watching the Evening News back at the hotel.

Two Feathers touches the screen and looks back and forth from Benny to the TV. Then he touches himself and the TV image.

Benny laughs. "You like television?"

"Television," Two Feathers says.

We watch the film of Two Feathers' sudden appearance on the runway. He just blinks in, exactly as we saw in the bowl.

"Move your hand, Two Feathers, so we can see it." Then Benny turns to me. "There! See that marker? That's it! That's what we need. I can find it now. He's about ten feet in front of the marker.

"We're all set!" I say.

Wednesday arrives. I turn the toys over to Benny in an official ceremony that involves stuffing them into the shoe box that Two Feathers' new boots came in and handing it to Benny, who tapes it up and slaps a mailing label on it addressed to his place of business.

I then stuff into the empty backpack everything that will travel back in time with Two Feathers. It now contains his and Benny's hospital clothes, new face paints, warm socks and leather gloves from Benny, 'for when it gets cold outside.'

Soon, it is time to go. We take a cab to the airport and go straight to the private terminal.

"Hey, Geoff," Benny says to the man at the counter.

"Al Bennington! Where you been, man? Everyone was worried after we saw the news report about you."

"I've been around."

"I heard your plane was stolen and crashed." Geoff says.

"I'm leasing one for today."

"Thank goodness for insurance." Geoff keys something into his computer.

"Yep. Gotta get me a new plane. I'll be back in a few days."

"Who ya got with you?" Geoff asks, looking at each of us and stopping at Two Feathers. "Is it Halloween already?"

"No. These are my — nephews."

Geoff looks skeptical.

"And niece," Nefertiti adds.

"Whatever you say, man." Geoff hands Benny some papers. "Have a nice trip."

We sit in the waiting area and Benny gets everyone a soft drink from the nearby machine. I check my watch. *One-thirty.* "I don't like this. The replacement is at two forty-seven. It's too close."

"It's perfect," Nefertiti says. "Will you relax?"

How will Jamie get to your time?" Benny asks.

Hearing his name, Jamie looks up from playing marbles.

"Umm," I look up at Dingus, who shrugs. "He won't," I say to Jamie.

"What?" Jamie stands up.

No sense putting it off any longer. I reach into my pocket and pull out the folded papers Dingus gave me yesterday. I hand them to Benny.

Benny unfolds them and reads the first one. "James Column... Bennington?" He looks up at me. "Are you kidding?"

Jamie leans in to see the papers.

"It's the only way," I say. "In our time, we use our fingerprints from when we're born. There won't be a match for him in our time and you can't reproduce something like that."

"So you expect me to run around with a fake birth certificate?"

"It's authentic," Dingus says, affronted. "Never underestimate my hacking skills. And in these primitive systems, it was a piece of cake."

"What exactly did you hack into?" Benny asks.

"The State of Illinois birth records and the United States Social Security office."

Benny checks the other paper. It's a Social Security card for *James Column Bennington*. "Haven't you gotten me into enough trouble already?"

"Trust me," Dingus says. "Jamie is now an official native of Illinois, born July 14, 1966. That makes him ten years old today!"

"All right, Jamie!" Nerfertiti says. "Happy birthday."

"I have a birthday?" He looks at Dingus.

"And a new dad," Dingus says.

"Aw, but, I'm not the fatherly type," Benny protests.

"Yes you are!" Dingus says. "You just don't know it."

"You'll do great, Benny," I say. "Besides, you both experienced something that you can never talk about with anyone else. Except each other."

"But he's a white boy. People will notice. I'm not even married. Who'd you name as the mother?" Benny reads the certificate. "Mother unknown?" He looks up at Dingus. "Uh, it doesn't quite work like that."

Dingus shrugs. "It was a computer system. It didn't ask questions."

"Just go with it," I say to Benny.

Jamie looks up at Benny with hope in his eyes.

"Aw... The things I do for fame and fortune. C'mon... *son*." Benny gives him a bear hug. "We'll fly the friendly skies together and invent the best toys ever!"

At two o'clock we each climb into our seats. Jamie sits up front next to Benny. Benny starts the engine and, when cleared to roll out, heads for the runway.

When we reach the runway, Benny points out the window. "Nikola, watch along that side. You see those markers?"

"Yeah."

"Tell Two Feathers to go all the way out to the last one, okay? The one on the left."

"Okay," I say.

"About ten feet this side of it," Benny adds.

"He can be close enough," Dingus says. "As long as no one else is around, the program can zero in on him."

We receive clearance to go. "Is everyone ready?" Benny says.

"Ready," a chorus rises up from all of us. I add a thumbs up. "Ready."

Benny rolls the plane out onto the runway, then stops and says into the mike, "Control, this is 483. Something's wrong with my plane. Over."

483, you're clear to go. What's the problem?

"483 here. Not sure. It's making a noise and it almost stalled just now. I'm not flying this plane with kids on board. I'm heading back. I'll have someone check it out and leave tomorrow. Over."

Affirmative 483. Come on back.

"Heading back. 483 out." Benny makes a wide turn into a shady spot on the field so that the door faces toward the fence and away from the hangar and tower. He stops the plane.

I get up with Two Feathers and fasten my watch to his wrist. "This is it." I speak into the translator to make sure he understands clearly. "I'm sorry we can't wait with you but we have to get to our own marks." I point to the watch. "You'll have to wait a while. Just lie in the shadow behind that shed. Do you see it?"

He nods.

"Good. When you hear the alarm on the watch, click this button to turn it off. Then walk out to that marker," I point toward the marker, "and count ten steps in front of it. Then just stand there and wait. It won't take long so be ready to blink back into your time. Do you understand?"

Two Feathers repeats the instructions and I have to accept that. I shake his hand. "Move quickly now or they'll get suspicious."

Nefertiti kisses him on the cheek, making Two Feathers blush. Benny, Jamie and Dingus shake his hand. He waives one last time before stepping off the plane. He crouches and rushes toward the shed to await his moment.

Benny slams the door shut and jumps back into the pilot's seat.

What's happening 483?

"Control, this is 483. I stalled again, but I got it going. On my way. Over."

Roger 483.

We return to the hanger and head for the hallway to find our markers.

I want Benny to stay and watch to make sure Two Feathers makes it okay, but everyone is against that. Dingus assures me we can check on him later. Besides, we may need Benny's help more since our original displacement point was in the air, possibly even inside the ceiling. If the "close-enough" rule truly applies, we should be okay if we can just get high enough above the floor. We shouldn't need to actually *be* inside the ceiling.

Earlier, we had stashed a couple of folding chairs near the corridor, so we grab them on the way in. I find my marker right beside Dingus'. Nefertiti's is just a few feet away. Nefertiti and I each plant our chairs on top of our markers. Dingus won't need one since I'll just turn him off for the trip home.

"So, this is it," I say to Jamie and my lips tremble. I realize suddenly that I'm never going to see my new friends again. This is a new feeling for me. It hurts right in my chest. It actually hurts! I cough to clear a scratchiness out of my throat. "You'll be okay with Benny."

Nefertiti is outright bawling. She lets Benny wrap her up in his big arms. When he lets go, she hugs Jamie while I shake Benny's hand.

"It's two forty six. One more minute," Dingus warns. He turns to me. "You *are* going home, right?"

"Yeah. I'm going," I say quietly. After Two Feathers' brave declaration and resolve to return to a real life-and-death battle, I'd never be able to face myself if I stay behind. "I'll see you on the flip side, okay?"

Dingus nods. I click him off.

Nefertiti steps up on her chair. I silently hope the chair idea works and that the "close-enough" rule holds true. I step up on my own chair, but I'm still shorter than Benny. Nefertiti raises her hands above her head and her fingers just touch the ceiling. But she wobbles when her folding chair begins to collapse. Jamie thrusts his knee on the chair, which helps to steady it. He wraps his arms around Nefertiti's legs. "Keep yer hands up," he says. "I've got ye."

"I'm not tall enough!" I say to Benny in a panic.

"I've got an idea." Benny lifts me at the waist and hoists me over his head. Sitting on Benny' shoulders, I can touch the ceiling too. Benny kicks the chair and it clatters away. He stands directly on the filthy sliver of tape that Dingus placed on the floor ten days earlier.

"Thanks," I say.

"Stop!" a familiar voice shouts from the end of the hallway.

My head jolts toward the sound. The lump in my throat threatens to spew out of my mouth. Pheloni races toward us and dives like a baseball player sliding into home plate.

"Noooooo!" I hear myself say as I fall into darkness.

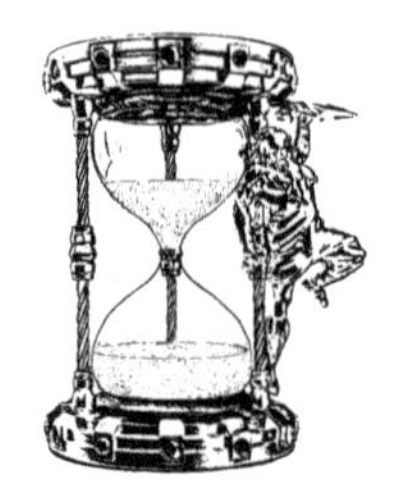

The final showdown

I am on the floor. Did Benny drop me? Yes. Benny must have fallen too because he's lying beside me. I look up.

Daemon!

Daemon is standing beside the table looking down at me. "Huh?" he murmurs. "This thing doesn't work."

The player's room! We made it. The tournament! My memory floods back into my head. I look around and see Nefertiti. Then I see Jamie too. And Pheloni! Pheloni is under the table holding onto Benny's leg.

I reach to my hip and feel for the button to turn Dingus back on.

"Dingus!" I say as soon as my friend appears. "Never mind food just now. We've got bigger problems."

Pheloni lets go of Benny's leg and starts to get up. But he hits his head on the underside of the table and falls back down. "Ow!" he shouts. That wakes Benny up. Everyone is beginning to stir. I jump to my feet and help Benny to move away from Pheloni.

But Pheloni gets up and looks around the room. "We're here, aren't we?"

"Where'd these guys come from?" Daemon says. "Who's that?" he asks, pointing at Pheloni.

"No one," Dingus says to Daemon. "Forget you saw them." He steps up to my compad, which is still on the table and types a few commands.

"What are you doing?" Pheloni says to Dingus.

"Sending you to where you can't cause any trouble. How does 1776 sound? Maybe the Potawatomi people will like you. Maybe they won't." Dingus points to each of the two calendars.

"Noooo!" Pheloni yells as he disappears.

"Where'd he go?" Daemon asked, stunned.

Dingus looks at me to answer. "Let Two Feathers and his people deal with him on their turf."

I'm about to react but a tournament official appears in the doorway. "Are you boys ready? It's time for your final match."

"No. Not yet!" Everything is happening too fast.

"What's going on?" Daemon demands. "Who are these people?"

"Just spectators," Nefertiti says.

"Come along, boys," the man at the door says. "Your public awaits."

My heart jolts. I look at Daemon. Then I hear the crowd roar as the announcer says our names.

Daemon sneers at me. "I'll see you in the arena!" He turns toward the door and leaves us.

"Go," Nefertiti urges me. "We'll be in the stands cheering for you." She kisses my cheek and takes Jamie's hand. "Come on." She looks at Benny and then Dingus. "They can stay for the match, can't they?"

Jamie looks up at Benny. Benny looks at me. "Are you kidding? I wouldn't miss this for all the toys in the twenty-first century. You can send us home after, okay?"

"Uh..." Somehow I managed to nod.

"Good luck, Buddy," Dingus slaps me on the shoulder. "We'll all be cheering for you."

I take a deep breath wishing I had more time to prepare. I follow everyone out to the arena.

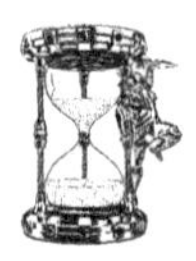

I have a sinking feeling just before they announce the game. *Please don't let it be …*

Gladiators!

I groan. The game had been predetermined long before the day's events. Probably the moment I was born. I've seen the ad for *Gladiators*. It's hand-to hand combat. And Daemon outweighs me by at least forty pounds. My only hope is to find ways to outsmart him.

Daemon sneers at me and steps a booted foot forward. I step back. Then I remember the required handshake and feel foolish. I swipe at a trickle of sweat from my forehead. Daemon stretches his hand toward me. I wipe my sweaty palm on my shorts before extending my arm for the handshake.

Daemon takes my hand and squeezes.

Hard.

I wince and try to pull away. Daemon's eyes meet mine and I'm drawn in as Daemon continues to crush my much smaller hand. I want to look away but I can't. Daemon holds on for a second longer and finally lets go.

I resist the urge to soothe the pain. Instead I let my hand fall, throbbing to my side. I step back.

Daemon puts on his earpiece. I do the same. I breathe in and out like I'm about to dive into a pool, stopping on the inhale. Then, I pull on my sensor gloves. I press the visual button on my earpiece and slowly let my breath out.

I'm standing on the gravel surface of the Roman Coliseum. When Daemon appears, I take a step back. I assume my outfit is similar to Daemon's – leather sandals, a short toga and leather breast armor. Daemon's helmet covers his head, but not his face. It has a single spike on the top.

I reach up to touch my head. I feel many spikes coming out in all directions of my own helmet.

I use my peripheral vision to get a sense of the arena while keeping an eye on Daemon's movements. I don't want to risk looking away from him, but I need a weapon quickly. According to the game's ad, weapons are scattered in the gravel. If I want a shield, I need to get a weapon first. I can use the weapon to draw a shape in the gravel and the shape will form into a shield.

But I don't get the chance to find a weapon or make a shield because Daemon charges at me and pushes me down. In an instant I'm on my back with Daemon sitting on my chest. He pounds his fists into my breast armor, over and over as he roars at me. I struggle to breathe. A virtual weapon can't hurt me, but Daemon is using real fists!

I turn my head away to avoid a blow to the face. Then I do the only thing that comes to my mind. I close my eyes against the blows, reach up and underneath Daemon's arms, find the soft spots, and pinch as hard as I can.

Daemon's aggressive bellows turn into a high-pitch scream. The storm of punches stops. I open my eyes and see that Daemon has fallen forward; his nose nearly touching mine. I head butt him with my spikey helmet and he rolls off.

I scrambled to my feet and run as fast as I can to the opposite side of the arena. Daemon closes the distance. I spot a short-handled axe and shift toward it. Daemon slows down as if allowing me time to pick up the axe.

Before I even lift it completely, I use it to draw a round circle in the gravel. The shield materializes instantly and I snatch that up with my other hand. When my eyes meet Daemon's, I see he now has both a spear and a sword. I must have run right past them in my haste to get away.

Daemon begins to circle around me, forcing me to do the same. Step by step I go one direction while he goes the other. I attempt to widen the circle to create more space between us while keeping an eye out for a better weapon. I succeed in enlarging the circle, but only until Daemon figures out what I'm doing. Then he begins to shrink it.

When we're about 15 feet apart, he raises the spear.

I raise my shield, wishing I had drawn a bigger one.

Daemon hurls the spear. It strikes the shield. I am forced back several steps by the impact. The point emerges just below my arm, but doesn't graze me. I have to struggle to hold the extra weight that's now attached to my shield. It's too heavy and the back of the spear drags in the gravel.

I have no time to pull the spear out. Daemon charges me again. In a panic, I drop both the spear and the shield and race to the far side of the arena. Daemon leaps over the spear and shield and continues toward me.

I use the axe to quickly draw a slightly larger shield. I pick it up and strap it to my arm.

Daemon frees the spear from my old shield. He tosses the shield away and strides toward me in a confident swagger. I can do nothing but wait for his arrival.

When Daemon is about ten feet away, I chuck the axe at him. I didn't think about doing it. It was a stupid reflexive move that I immediately regret. Daemon dips his shoulder to let the axe sail harmlessly past him. And now I have no weapon.

He wraps both hands around the spear like a baseball bat and takes several steps toward me like he's stepping up to home plate. When he swings the spear, he hits a home run and I land on my back. My arms and legs splay in different directions. Daemon tosses the spear aside. In slow motion, he pulls the sword from his belt. He steps on my shield which pins my arm to the ground. Then he points the sword at my chest.

I try to swallow but my throat is dry.

Daemon wraps both hands dramatically around the hilt.

I see the image of Two Feathers under his attacker's blade. Two Feathers had been inches from actual death. Daemon's blade will pass harmlessly through me. This is just a game and I will live to play again.

Then I remember Father Serra's words. *Attack your enemy by befriending him.*

"W... Why can't we be friends?" I say in a weak voice.

Daemon looks surprised. "What?"

"I'm no threat to you... clearly." I hear my own voice, barely a whisper.

Daemon raises the sword.

"Nooooooo!" I recognize Jamie's shout from the audience seeping into the game. Jamie had played Viarbox. He should understand it's just a game. *Game!* I remember Jamie's marble game. I remember Father Serra's story about the boy who defeated the warrior with just a sling shot. I remember how I had hit Pheloni with the yo-yo.

"What do you say?" I keep eye contact as I talk to Daemon. "It's over. You won. I lost. It was a good game. We can end it as friends." As I'm speaking, I fumble in the dirt with my free hand.

"No way." Daemon answers, his teeth still clenched.

"Why not?" I continue.

"Friends?" Daemon shakes his head.

"We both like to play Viarbox." I pinch a good-sized pebble between my thumb and forefinger. "Is this about what happened at Eniac's yesterday?"

Daemon raises the sword higher. "Now you'll see how it feels to be laughed at." As Daemon is about to thrust the sword, I flick the stone the way Jamie taught me.

It slaps loudly just above the bridge of Daemon's nose.

Daemon blinks. Then ever so slowly, his eyes roll up and he falls on his back with a crash.

I jump to my feet and grab the sword from Daemon's unresisting hand. Daemon opens his eyes and our roles are now reversed. I am pointing the sword at Daemon's neck.

"I don't want people to laugh at you. Or me," I whisper down to him. "I'll let you win if you promise to back off. Be my friend or leave me alone after today."

Daemon's mouth forms in a tight line. He doesn't answer.

"Say you will and I'll let you win."

Daemon stares up at me. When I see his infinitesimal nod, I whisper, "Sweep my leg and I'll go down."

Daemon doesn't hesitate. He grabs my ankle and yanks. I fall onto my back. I don't fight back when Daemon jumps up and snatches the sword. I don't resist when Daemon thrusts the sword into my belly.

The audience erupts into whoops and cheers. I press the visual button near my temple and am lying on my back in the stadium arena.

A man helps me up and escorts me off the floor. Another official carries the four-foot tall trophy to the center of the arena. I think for a brief moment as he passes that it could have been mine. Instead he hands it to Daemon.

"Why?" Dingus says for the umpteenth time. I've never seen Dingus look more disappointed.

"I didn't want to give him another reason to hate me. Do you think he'd ever leave me alone if I had won? Besides, this is his final year. I've got two more years to try again. And maybe he and I really can be friends."

"You don't really believe that, do you? I mean..." Dingus slaps his chest. "I'm your friend!"

I smile. "Yeah. You're my best friend, Dingus." I pat his shoulder and turn to my *other* friends, Nefertiti, Benny and Jamie. "A guy can have more than one friend."

"But... he'll bring Kluge with him!" Dingus whines, now behind me.

I look over my shoulder at him. "Don't worry, Ding. I've got your back."

Dingus, Nefertiti, Benny, Jamie and I find a secluded nook in the lobby to say goodbye. "Thanks for staying. I'm glad you were here," I say to Benny and Jamie. And I mean it. I'm euphoric, even though I lost.

"I'm proud of you," Benny says, making me blush. "I wouldn't have missed this for the world."

We all hug and shake hands once again. Finally, Benny puts his arm around Jamie's shoulder and, at my nod, Dingus sends them to 1976.

Nefertiti, Dingus and I walk out of the nook and into the crowded lobby, heading toward the carnival outside.

As we flow along in the sea of people, Dingus comes to an abrupt halt. I stop next to him and someone bumps into my back. Nefertiti stops on his other side. The wave of people reroutes itself around us.

"What?" I say.

Dingus turns his face to me and smiles. His ears turn pink and his grin broadens. He slaps himself in the forehead.

"Dingus, what is it?" Nefertiti says.

"Ohmagosh!" Dingus says and he laughs. He fumbles in his pocket and pulls out my compad. Then he unfolds it and stoops to place it on the tiled floor in front of us. We all squat down right in the middle of the crowd. Flicking the hourglass icon, Dingus calls up the code. With inhuman speed, he finds what he's looking for.

I look around at the crowd, but no one is paying attention to us.

"The name..." Dingus says, panting.

"What name?" Nefertiti says.

Dingus searches line after line of code in the *Displace* program. "The name... it just hit me... I remember...like it didn't exist until just now."

"What?" I say. "What didn't exist? What name?"

Dingus reaches into the code and pulls out the *Displace* program's author's line. It reads simply:

James C. Bennington.

Thank you for reading!

Authors love hearing from their readers! Please let JJ Carroll know what you thought about *Displaced: Both Feet in the Game* by leaving a short review on Amazon or your other preferred online store. It will help other parents and kids find the story.

If you're under age 13, ask a grown up to help you. Not sure what to write in a book review? Don't worry, it can be short. You can tell us which was your favorite scene or character and why. (Be careful not to give away the ending.)

Be first to learn about more books from JJ Carrol

Visit JJCarrollBooks.com.

Research Notes

While writing this book, I traveled to Chicago, Philadelphia, and San Diego and visited each one of the sites that became the various settings for this book.

Unfortunately, I neglected to write down the names of those very helpful people who gave me special tours, and took time to share knowledge of histories and nuances of the locations to me. In my defense, these things happened many years ago, before I knew I would have a published book on my hands. But, as I hope to make this a series, I promise to do better next time. I do apologize and, in my heart if not in public, I thank each and every one of those very special helpers.

Cook County Hospital

During my visit to the present-day Cook County Hospital, I had the pleasure of speaking with a security guard who had worked at the hospital for some time and remembered the old secure ward, which no longer exists. He explained that the former "A" building, would have held Cook County Jail prisoners who needed medical attention. The secure ward was on the 7th floor; therefore I made up "A723" as the room number where Benny and Two Feathers were held. The building was eventually torn down, so all other descriptions are from my imagination.

Arch Street Friends Meeting House

The meeting house where our characters spent two nights in 1976 is situated at 4th and Arch Streets in "Old City" Philadelphia.

The land on which the building sits was donated to the Society of Friends by William Penn in 1701. The cemetery would have existed in Jamie's time. But, the building wasn't constructed until 1804, many years after he left, as Nefertiti mentions in the story.

I visit Old City Philly as often as I can. It's one of my favorite places to be. And I've been to the meeting house several times and was given a special tour during one of my visits. Everything I said about the meeting house is true, from the cloak-room with lost-and-found coats and sweaters, to the trap-door hiding space. The cushions on the pews really are hard and sort of crunchy. It's because the stuffing is made of horse hair. It's also the original stuffing from when the meeting house was first built. That makes it over 200 years old! Only the outside coverings of the cushions get replaced as needed.

Learn more about The Arch Street Friends Meeting House at www.ushistory.org/tour/arch-street-friends.htm.

Father Serra and the San Diego de Alcalá Mission

Father Junipero Serra was a real person who became a monk when he was 16 years old. That may sound young today, but was pretty normal in his time.

He was born in Spain in 1713. After becoming a Franciscan monk, he moved to Mexico to establish new missions and preach to the natives. He was 54 years old when he was appointed to build the missions in California. San Diego de Alcalá Mission was the first one. He eventually built nine of 21 missions along the Pacific coast and baptized over 6,000 Native Americans, playing a major role in developing what would become present day California.

Father Serra knew about and supported the colonists' war for independence. He even took up a collection from his mission parishes and sent it to help General Washington.

When Pope Francis visited the United States in 2015, he "canonized" Father Serra, which means Father Serra is now considered a saint in the eyes of Catholics. It was the first time a saint was canonized in America.

My research for Father Serra and the San Diego mission included a personal tour of the site and museum, purchasing print materials at the site, and internet research. I find there is some confusion, or perhaps simply a lack of clarity, of Father Serra's whereabouts in July of 1776.

Father Serra founded San Diego de Alcalá Mission in 1769 before heading north to establish other missions. The original San Diego mission was later attacked and burned to the ground by local natives. Father Serra returned to the site in 1776 to rebuild, but no exact date is given. Therefore, he may have been in San Diego, or he may have been at the San Juan Capistrano mission, which he founded on November 1, 1776. I took creative license to place him at the San Diego mission on July 4, 1776.

Learn more about San Diego de Alcalá Mission at: www.missionscalifornia.com/missions/san-diego-de-alcala.

Learn more about Father Junipero Serra at: www.sfmuseum.net/bio/jserra.html.

About the Author

JJ Carroll is the curator of **HistoricBooksForKids.com**. She's also a voracious reader of anything time travel or history related for any period or place. She especially loves living in Pennsylvania because it is right smack in the middle of U.S. history.

JJ and her husband are empty nesters, happily living within ten minutes of all three of their children and many grandchildren. And that gives her more joy than reading or writing, or even things that are yellow!

Be sure to visit **HistoricBooksForKids.com**

- Download free stuff like puzzles, games, ebooks and more.
- Read interesting articles about historic topics
- Find pre-reviewed kids' fiction and nonfiction books about different times in history (with and without time travel)